Praise for
BOYS AGAINST GIRLS

"Fast-paced. . . . Fans of the previous books will enjoy this installment." —*School Library Journal*

"Entertaining, and the writing is ever lively." —*The Bulletin of the Center for Children's Books*

PHYLLIS REYNOLDS NAYLOR

BOYS AGAINST GIRLS

SCHOLASTIC INC.

New York Toronto London Auckland Sydney
Mexico City New Delhi Hong Kong Buenos Aires

ISBN-13: 978-0-439-89405-0
ISBN-10: 0-439-89405-0

Copyright © 1994 by Phyllis Reynolds Naylor.
All rights reserved. Published by Scholastic Inc.,
557 Broadway, New York, NY 10012, by arrangement with Random House Children's Books, a division of Random House, Inc. SCHOLASTIC and associated logos are trademarks and/or registered trademarks of Scholastic Inc.

12   13 14 15 16 17/0

Printed in the U.S.A.   40

First Scholastic printing, January 2007

*To the people at Oldakers' Bookstore
in Buckhannon, West Virginia,
which is almost, but not quite,
where this story takes place*

Contents

▽ • ▽ • ▽ • ▽ • ▽

BOYS AGAINST GIRLS

▽ • ▽ • ▽ • ▽ • ▽

▽ • ▽ • ▽ • ▽ • ▽ • ▽ • ▽ • ▽ • ▽ • ▽ • ▽

One

▽

Abaguchie

Wally Hatford usually spent the day after Halloween counting his trick-or-treat candy, trading off Mars bars for Milky Ways, and opening all the little packets of candy corn. He'd pop a whole handful into his mouth at once, and follow that with a couple of chocolate kisses.

But not this Halloween.

Wally and his two older brothers, Jake and Josh, sat numbly in the living room, looking at the candy wrappers scattered about the floor after their party for the girls—the party the Malloy girls had tricked them into giving. Never mind that the Hatford brothers had tried to trap them in the cemetery and would have dropped worms on their heads if they'd succeeded. The fact that the girls had found them out and beaten them at their own game was too humiliating for words.

1

"You know what I wish?" said Jake after a while. "I just wish a big tornado would sweep through Buckman and blow them away. Not kill them, exactly—just deposit them back in Ohio where they belong."

"I wish there would be a big flood and they'd just wash away," said Josh, his eleven-year-old twin.

Seven-year-old Peter was eating a malted milk ball he'd found under the couch. He'd had no part in the trickery, so his conscience was clear. "What do *you* wish, Wally?" he asked.

Wally wished, quite frankly, that his brothers would quit asking him questions, that's what. He *always* got dragged into things whether he wanted to be or not. And right now he did not want to be.

He was tired of girls. Sick of girls. Bored to death with talking about them. Since the Hatfords' best friends had moved to Georgia and rented out their house to the Malloys, it had been "the Malloy girls this" and "the Malloy girls that," and if Jake and Josh hated them so much, why were they always talking about them, looking at them, laughing at them, and thinking about what they were going to do next? It was disgusting.

"Well?" said Jake and Josh together, still waiting for his answer.

Wally had to say something. He sighed. "I wish the abaguchie would carry them off," he said finally.

"That's *it*!" cried Jake. "Wally, you're a genius! It's perfect!"

Wally stretched his nine-year-old self out on the couch and stared up at the ceiling where the cracks in the plaster spread outward from around the light fixture. He wondered why it was you never saw a crack happening. Not once in his life had he been looking at a wall or ceiling and seen it crack. One morning he would be eating his Corn Chex and the wall would be fine. The next morning he would be eating his Corn Chex and there would be a thin hairline crack in the plaster.

"How are you going to get the abaguchie to come and carry off Caroline and her sisters?" asked Peter, wide eyed.

"All we're going to do is scare them a little," said Josh.

"Scare them a *lot*!" said Jake, and he and Josh laughed.

Actually, nobody knew if there was an abaguchie in Buckman at all, and if there was, just what kind of creature it was. For several years various people in Upshur County claimed to have seen a large animal, something like a cat, lurking around in the shadows, running along the edge of the woods, or even crawling about under somebody's window.

Tracks were supposedly found in the dirt, howls were heard in the night—more like "squawls," someone said—and sometimes a chicken or cat or a dog was found half eaten. Two different farmers even complained that one of their calves was missing. The newspaper would report these incidents, and everyone would talk about the abaguchie awhile. Then the people of Buckman would lose interest until it happened all over again.

"So we tell the girls about the abaguchie. So what?" Wally said.

"So they'll get scared. *Real* scared. And we'll just sort of help things along," Jake told him. "Monday, in school, you tell Caroline."

Wally bolted straight up. "Oh, no! Don't get me messed up in this. If you want to scare the girls, *you* tell them."

"Wally, you've got to!" said Jake. "If we tell Eddie or Beth, they'll never believe us. Old Caroline will believe *any*thing. You know that. And if we can make Caroline believe it, she'll tell her sisters."

It was going to be like this forever and ever, Wally knew. Unless the Bensons came back at the end of the year, the Malloys would probably stay in Buckman, and Wally would have to listen to his brothers talk about them for the rest of his life. The Benson boys were the best friends the Hatfords had ever had. Why their father had decided to take a job in Georgia for a year, Wally could not understand. But they had rented their house to the Malloys and, what's worse, they seemed to be enjoying it down in Georgia.

When he went to bed that night, Wally thought about how he did not want to have to get involved with the girls again.

When he got up the next morning, he thought about how the last thing in the world he wanted to hear was anything at all about the Malloys.

But when he saw the three girls coming across the swinging bridge toward College Avenue and Buckman Elementary, he imagined how Caroline's eyes would grow big as cantaloupes when he told her about the abaguchie, and he found himself smiling.

It was a cold November day, and only a few stubborn leaves clung to the tree limbs. It took a long while for the West Virginia sun to get up over the rim of the hills and warm the sidewalks, and then it was down again before you knew it, slipping and sliding behind the courthouse.

The Buckman River shone silver in the early morning light where it looped around at the end of Island Avenue and came flowing back again. When you rode into Buckman for the first time, right out to the end of Island Avenue and over the bridge into the business district, you might not realize that the river on your right was the same as the river on your left, and before you knew it, you'd be passing City

Hall and the police department and the college campus.

Wally hung up his jacket, clunked his lunch box on the shelf overhead, and slouched on into the classroom.

Caroline Malloy was there, of course, in the desk right behind his, and she looked fatter. Yes, he was sure of it. Her cheeks were just a little bit puffier than they were before, and Wally was sure it was because his very own Milky Way bars and M&M's were in her stomach instead of his. All because the girls told Mom that the boys had invited them to a Halloween party, and Mom made him and Josh and Jake share all the candy they had collected. His stomach growled more out of anger than hunger.

Maybe he *would* like Caroline to think that there was a creature called an abaguchie around. Maybe he *would* like to see her looking over her shoulder as she went back and forth to school. She wasn't even supposed to be in fourth grade at all, she was supposed to be in third. Just because she was supposed to be super smart—"precocious," the grown-ups called it—didn't mean he had to like her. Wally began to think that precocious was just about the most awful thing you could possibly be, next to dead.

Everyone was talking about Halloween—what they had done and where they had gone—and when

Caroline finally settled down, Wally turned around and said, "You don't have any pets, do you?"

"What?" said Caroline. Even her neck was fatter, Wally decided. She had probably spent the whole weekend eating Wally's candy.

"Pets. Cats or dogs or rabbits or anything."

"No. Why?"

"Oh, nothing," said Wally, and turned back around again.

Caroline grabbed at his sweater and tugged. *"Why?"* she insisted.

Wally half turned. "Because the abaguchie's been seen again."

"What?"

Wally turned completely around this time. "Hasn't anyone told you about the abaguchie?"

"What are you talking about?"

"It's some kind of animal. Except no one knows what, so we just call it the abaguchie here in Buckman. Every so often someone sees it around dark, and the newspaper has another story. They say it carries off pets and stuff."

Caroline's eyes got as dark as her hair, which she wore in a long ponytail. "You're just making that up."

Wally shrugged. "Don't believe me, then. I don't care. Ask anyone. You can even look it up in old newspapers."

He turned toward the front of the room again as Miss Applebaum rapped for attention. But as the homework papers were being collected later, Wally felt another tug on his sweater, and heard Caroline whisper, "Does it ever attack people?"

"Hasn't yet," he whispered over his shoulder. "But it's carried off some hundred-pound calves. You won't find many people sitting out on their steps alone after dark." And when he faced forward again, Wally had to be very, very careful that a smile didn't take over his whole face.

Two

▽

Call of the Wild

The very first thing that entered Caroline Malloy's head when she heard about the abaguchie was what a marvelous movie it would make. That would be the title, of course: just *Abaguchie*.

While the credits were rolling across the screen, the camera would be scanning a typical small-town neighborhood about dusk, zooming in on a young girl sitting on the steps of her house with a kitten in her lap, watching the sky grow dark, the fireflies come out, and the moon rise up in the sky.

After a while she would feel chilly, so she'd put down her kitten and go inside to get a sweater, and when she came back, the kitten would be gone. Worse yet, on the steps where the kitten had been, there would be . . . Yes! A pool of blood. And a little tuft of white fur, along with the kitten's collar. And the girl's eyes would open wider and wider. She would grab her throat and stifle a scream, and then . . . in big letters filling up the whole screen, *ABAGUCHIE, starring Caroline Lenore Malloy.*

"Caroline, what the heck?" asked her oldest sister, Eddie, as the girls walked home from school, and it was only then that Caroline realized she was walking down the sidewalk clutching her throat. Caroline's one ambition in life was to be an actress, and an actress, as everyone knows, always has an eye out for a good role.

"How did I look just then?" Caroline asked eagerly. "Horrified? Frightened? Stunned? What?"

"You looked like you were about to throw up," said Beth, the middle daughter in the Malloy family.

Caroline looked at her ten- and eleven-year-old sisters. "I was just thinking about what it would be like if I found a pool of blood and a little tuft of white fur where I'd left my kitten. If I *had* a kitten."

Eddie gave her a peculiar look, lifted the baseball cap she wore all the time on her head, and put it on again backward. "Sometimes I wonder about you, Caroline, I really do."

But Beth was more sympathetic. Beth always had her nose stuck in a book, *Zombies on the Loose* or *The Smell of Midnight* or something, so she understood things like pools of blood and tufts of fur.

"What got you thinking about that?" Beth asked.

"Wally Hatford asked me if we had pets. He said if

we did, we'd better not leave them outside after dark, because the abaguchie had been seen again."

"The what?" asked Eddie. Eddie's name was really Edith Ann, but she hated it, and preferred Eddie.

"That's what he called it. He said nobody knows what kind of animal it is, so people around here call it the abaguchie. It comes out around dusk and several people have seen it. He said there had just been another sighting."

"Spookie!" breathed Beth.

But Eddie scoffed. "That sounds exactly like something those Hatford goons would dream up! Caroline, can't you tell when somebody's pulling your leg?"

"He said we could look it up in old newspapers, that there had been stories written about it."

"Oh," said Eddie, and grew thoughtful.

•

At dinner that evening Caroline was thinking some more about the movie she was creating in her mind when she suddenly wondered what would play the part of the kitten. *No* one would want a real kitten to be snatched up by some creature and squeezed and clawed to death. Then she realized that a little kitten didn't have to die at all to leave a little blood and fur behind. All you needed was a close-up of a kitten sitting peacefully on the steps in the dark, and in the next shot you could have a pool of fake blood and a piece of fuzz off a wool blanket or something.

She put a spoonful of strawberry jelly on her plate and stirred it around with a fork. Too light. She poured a little catsup in it and mixed some more. That looked somewhat more like blood, but perhaps if she—

"Caroline, what on earth are you doing?" asked her father.

"Making blood," Caroline told him. "For my death-of-a-kitten scene."

"Your what?" came Mother's voice.

So Caroline had to explain once again what Wally Hatford had told her about the abaguchie.

"That sounds like absolute nonsense," Mother said.

"Well, I've heard the faculty mention it once or twice," Father said. He was coaching the college football team this year, and wasn't quite sure whether he would stay on after the year was over or move the family back to Ohio. "I've heard different players on the team joke about it now and then too."

"Then that's the last time I'm going to go for firewood after dark," Mother said.

"Could be some bobcat or something, but from what the faculty members say, it's supposed to be bigger. Probably like the Loch Ness monster—the more you talk about it, the bigger it gets," Father said.

·

There was a PTA meeting the following night, and both Mr. and Mrs. Malloy got ready to go.

"Anything special you want us to ask your teachers?" Mother said, throwing on her jacket.

"Could you ask when the next school play will be?" Caroline begged. "I'll just die if I have to wait until fifth grade to be in another play."

"Ask when I can try out for the softball team," Eddie told her father. "They said March, but I see guys out there practicing all the time, and I want to be sure they don't hold tryouts without me."

"Ask why we can't have silent reading at our desks like we did back in Ohio," Beth suggested. "I could finish a book in two days if we just had silent reading in school."

"We'll ask," said Mother, and she and Father headed outside and down the bank toward the swinging bridge, to walk the few blocks to Buckman Elementary.

Eddie and Beth spread their homework out on the dining-room table and began their assignments, while Caroline stretched out on the sofa with her geography book and tried to memorize the capitals of the states west of the Mississippi.

The fire in the fireplace snapped and popped occasionally, and now and then there would be a clunk as another log fell, smoking and sizzling. She recited under her breath:

> *"North Dakota, Bis-marck,*
> *South Dakota, Pierre;*
> *Nebras-ka, Lin-coln,*
> *Kan-sas, To-peka."*

Suddenly she put down her geography book and listened.

There was a soft distant sound of . . . well, she wasn't sure. A moan? Like something in pain, perhaps?

She lifted her head from the cushion and looked at Beth and Eddie.

Another moan, more like a howl this time. A moaning howl. A howling moan. Closer now. Was it anything they had ever heard before? She didn't think so.

Beth and Eddie had heard it too.

Caroline swung her legs over the side of the couch and sat up. They listened some more.

Again the noise came. More like an animal, Caroline thought, but no animal she could name. It was growing louder all the time.

All three girls ran to the dining-room window overlooking the Buckman River below, hands cupped over their eyes to search out the darkness, ears listening for the least little sound.

"Owl-oooo! Owl-oooo!" came the noise again. Then a sort of yipping, yelping sound, followed by another "Owl-oooo!"

Beth's voice was shaky. "Eddie, what *is* it?"

"I don't know. It's not far away, whatever it is," Eddie said.

"Should we—should we call Mom and Dad at the school and ask them to come home?" asked Caroline, now frightened out of her wits.

"Or the police, maybe," said Beth.

"Owl-oooo! Yip, yip! Owl-oooo!" came the sound.

Caroline clung to Beth.

There was a grunting, scrabbling sound, like a creature snuffing and digging just outside the window; then the "owl-oooo" came once again.

"A-are all the windows locked?" asked Caroline.

"Never mind the windows; what about the doors?" asked Eddie. "Beth, go check."

"You come with me," said Beth, and her voice sounded unnaturally high.

Huddled together, the girls moved toward the front door and checked it, then started toward the kitchen.

"Owl-oooo! Owl-oooo!"

"Wait a minute. . . ." Eddie stood perfectly still. "Don't make a sound."

Caroline and Beth froze.

"Owl-oooo! Yip, yip, yip!"

"Listen," said Eddie. "Along about here there should be a whine."

Caroline stared at Eddie. They listened some more.

"Owl-oooo! Yip! . . . Owl-oooo! Yip! Yip!" And then, just as Eddie said, a whine.

Caroline's mouth dropped open.

"I *know* those sounds!" Eddie told them. "That's a cassette tape of *Wolves in the Wild*. We had to listen to that in science class last year in Ohio. We had to listen to that so much, I know it by heart."

"It's the Hatford boys!" said Caroline.

"*Them!*" said Beth.

Caroline didn't know whether she was more angry or excited. Every time the boys did something to them, it just gave the girls an excuse to do something worse.

"What are we going to do?" asked Beth.

"Leave the curtains open just like they are. You two run around inside and act scared," Eddie told them. "I'm going to sneak out and catch them when they go back down the driveway."

Three

▽

Bunny Slippers

Mr. and Mrs. Hatford went to the PTA meeting, too, and Wally had thought that for once in his life, perhaps, he could eat Fritos and watch TV first and do his homework later. He had his hand halfway into the sack of Fritos when Jake said, "Come on, we're going!"

"Where?" Wally was square shaped, with thick hands like his dad's. He and Peter resembled each other, while Jake and Josh were string-bean skinny, tall, and were tan by the first week of June. Even in November they seemed to look tan. "*Where* are we going?" Wally asked again.

In answer Jake held up a little rectangular box, and when Wally still didn't get it, he held up a cassette player.

"A cassette?"

Jake grinned and so did Josh, who was putting on his jacket in the hallway.

"What is it?" asked Wally.

"Wolves," said Jake. "Remember that tape Aunt Ida sent for our birthday—from the Wildlife Fund?" He read the label on the cassette. *"Wolves in the Wild.* We're going to play it outside the girls' window."

Wally grinned, too, and went for his jacket. Then he stopped. "What about Peter?"

Peter was sitting in front of the TV in his pajamas and bunny slippers, eating a box of Cracker Jack. Wally knew without asking that they were never, ever, to go off and leave Peter alone, especially at night.

"Darn! I forgot!" Jake paused, then went on into the living room. "Hey, Peter, want to go for a walk with us?"

"Huh-uh." Peter pressed the palm of his hand to his mouth as he devoured another fistful of Cracker Jack.

"Hey, come *on*! It'll be exciting!"

"No. I want to watch this," said Peter.

Josh and Wally went into the living room too.

"That's a rerun, Peter! You can see that any day! We're going to do something fun!" said Josh.

"What?"

"We're going to be wolves," said Jake.

Peter looked doubtful.

"We'll buy you three more boxes of Cracker Jack if you'll come," Jake promised.

Peter reluctantly slid off the couch, put on his jacket, and the four boys went out onto the porch and down the steps.

The thing was, Wally was thinking, Peter might tell. Letting Peter in on a secret was like putting water in a paper bag. Still, there was nothing to be done except tell him the truth. So when Peter asked Wally what they were going to do exactly, Wally answered:

"It's just a little joke, but we want to keep it secret, okay? Jake has that tape of wolves howling—you know the one Aunt Ida sent him? We're going to play it outside the Malloys' window so the girls will think it's the abaguchie."

Peter grinned a little. Wally could see his face under the streetlight. They crossed the road and started across the swinging footbridge that connected College Avenue to Island Avenue.

By the time they got all the way across, however, the bridge bouncing with every step, Peter complained that his feet hurt.

"He's still wearing his bunny slippers!" Jake said in dismay.

"I'll carry him," said Wally, and squatted down so

that Peter could climb on his back. He grabbed hold of Peter's legs, and they started off again.

At the foot of the Malloys' driveway, however, Wally set Peter down on a big rock there by the road.

"Now, you sit here and be very, very quiet," Wally told him.

"We're just going up to the window and play some of the tape, then we're coming right back and heading home," Jake said.

"Yeah, we want you to tell us what it sounds like from back here," said Josh.

"Okay." Peter pulled his feet up on the rock and circled his legs with his arms.

Wally, Jake, and Josh crept silently up the driveway. They went over to the lighted window.

Beth and Eddie were at the dining-room table, their schoolbooks spread out before them. And there in the living room was Caroline, sprawled on the couch, a book in her lap.

No mother in sight. No father. Just as the boys suspected, the girls were home alone.

The Hatfords crouched in the bushes just outside the dining-room window.

"Put it on medium volume to start, and then slowly increase it, as though the wolves are coming closer and closer," whispered Josh. "Maybe they've got the TV on."

Jake pushed up the volume control a little, then

pressed the "play" button. There came the low hiss of the tape, and then a loud "Owl-oooooo!"

At first nothing happened. But as Jake increased the volume and a third, and then a fourth "Owl-ooooo!" pierced the air, Wally saw Beth and Eddie look up, listening.

"Owl-oooo! Owl-oooo!"

Inside, the girls were talking to each other and looking toward the living room. Then Caroline, looking scared, appeared in the doorway of the dining room. All three were obviously listening.

"Owl-oooo! Owl-oooo! Yip, yip, yip!"

"Look! They're going nuts!" laughed Jake. "Did you see the way Caroline grabbed Beth?"

"Beth will pass out," wheezed Josh. "She reads those kinds of books all the time at recess. All you have to do is creep up behind her and she yells bloody murder."

"Owl-oooo! Yip, yip . . . Owl-oooo! Yip!"

"They're checking to make sure all the doors are locked," said Wally, choking with laughter.

"This is better than a circus!" cried Jake. "I'd bet my last dollar that Caroline came home with the story about the abaguchie and told the whole family. She's probably been worried about it ever since."

"How much longer are we going to stay out here? They might get suspicious," whispered Josh.

"What we've got to do is move around. If we stay

at one window too long they might figure it out. We'll go around to the other side and play it, like there's an animal circling the house, then leave," said Jake.

They moved on around the far side of the house. Inside, Beth dashed past the window, her face terrified. Then Caroline. The Malloy sisters were going crazy!

After a while Wally said, "What if they call someone, Jake? I mean, what if they call the police? We'd better clear out."

"What we ought to do is move slowly away from the house, like the abaguchie's going back into the woods. Let the howls sort of die away gradually," said Josh.

They moved around to the dining room again, then backed away, until at last they were at the foot of the driveway.

"Okay, now we've got to beat it," said Jake, turning the cassette player off. "Come on, Peter, let's go."

Wally made his way over to the big rock so that Peter could climb on his back again. Except that Peter was gone. Nothing was there on the rock but the tail off one of his bunny slippers.

∇ • ∇ • ∇ • ∇ • ∇ • ∇ • ∇ • ∇ • ∇ • ∇ • ∇ • ∇

Four

∇

Kidnapped

It was better than being in a play at school. Better even than being an actress onstage. On a stage or on the screen people knew it was just a story being acted out. But here, in a lighted window, in front of the Hatford boys, who were undoubtedly watching from out in the bushes somewhere, Caroline's role was to convince the boys that she was really, truly terrified.

She called upon everything she had ever learned about being frightened. In fact, whenever she was angry or embarrassed, frightened or sad, she turned it into something to remember—how it felt in her chest. Was her brow furrowed? Were her lips pursed? Her eyes squinting or open wide?

However she found herself, she added it to her memory bank, and now she brought forth everything she knew and played the role of being frightened for all it was worth.

"Oh, Beth! What will we do? What will we do?" she cried, putting panic in her voice and ending with a sob.

She had to admit that Beth played her part well, too, for her older sister rushed from room to room, hand to her throat, and every time a new "Owl-ooooo!" came from outside the window, they clutched at each other.

After five or six minutes, however, the wolf cries grew fainter and fainter until they were gone entirely. Caroline and Beth turned out the light in the living room and sat on the couch where the boys couldn't see them, shrieking with laughter.

"You were terrific, Beth! Really! Your face looked so worried!" Caroline said.

"And the way we ran around locking doors and windows!" said Beth.

There was the sound of someone fumbling with the back-door knob, then a knock.

"Should we answer?" asked Beth.

"Could be Eddie," said Caroline, and ran to open it.

There stood Peter Hatford in his bunny slippers, Eddie right behind him.

"Hi," he said. "Eddie invited me in for some root beer."

Caroline stared.

"Yes," said Eddie, ushering Peter on into the kitchen and winking at Beth and Caroline. "I went outside for a little walk, and happened to find Peter sitting on a rock at the end of our driveway. Seems as though his brothers left him there, so we decided to play a little joke on them. We hid in the bushes, and after they went home, I invited Peter in for some root beer."

"Oh, sure! One root beer coming up!" said Caroline, and went to the refrigerator.

"How about some ice cream in it?" asked Beth. "Did you ever have a root-beer float?"

Peter nodded eagerly, and within minutes a large glass of foaming root beer and ice cream was set in front of him, with a plastic straw. Peter drank with loud gulps and swallows, stopping occasionally to grin and wipe the back of his hand across his mouth.

Beth fixed floats for the rest of them and they sat with Peter around the table. Caroline studied the Hatfords' little brother. He was seven and she was eight, but he was a young seven and she was *almost* nine. She always felt like a much-older sister when she was around Peter.

"Do you and your brothers always sneak around outside after dark, Peter?" she asked.

Peter shook his head, his cheeks sunken as he sucked hard on the straw, taking the glass in both hands. "Only sometimes," he said at last.

"What exactly were you trying to do?" Beth quizzed him.

"I wasn't doing anything, just sitting," said Peter.

"Well, what were your brothers trying to do, then?"

"Just . . . um . . . playing," said Peter. "Making noises and stuff."

"What were they playing?" asked Caroline. Even though she and her sisters knew exactly what the boys had been up to, it was delicious getting Peter to spill the beans.

Peter didn't answer.

"Wolf, I'll bet," said Beth.

Peter stopped slurping and looked up. "How did you know?"

"Just a guess," said Beth. "What did they do? Take you with them and then forget all about you?"

"Yeah, that's what they did!" said Peter brightly. "Wally set me down on that rock, and he said to stay there until they . . . uh . . ."

"Until they what?" asked Eddie.

"Until they came back."

The phone rang. More smiles. Beth got up and answered. It was Wally's voice on the end of the line, and she held the receiver out away from her so that Caroline and Eddie could hear too:

"This is Wally. Listen, have you seen Peter?"

Beth turned toward the others there at the table and put her finger to her lips. Caroline and Eddie motioned to Peter not to make a sound.

"What are you talking about?" Beth asked.

Now there was panic in Wally's voice. Caroline *almost* felt sorry for him, but not quite.

"Are you *sure* you don't know where he is?" Wally bleated.

"Can't you even keep track of your own brother?" asked Beth. "I'll bet you guys were supposed to be sitting Peter and forgot all about him."

"We did not! We told him—I mean, the last we saw him, he was—"

"Sorry," said Beth, and hung up.

The three girls broke into laughter. Even Peter was smiling as his straw sucked noisily at the root beer in the bottom of his glass.

"Boy, Wally's gonna be sorry he left me on that rock," he said.

The phone rang again. This time it was Jake.

"Listen, if Peter's over there, you'd better tell me," he demanded.

"What would he be doing over here? He's probably supposed to be in bed!" said Beth. "Have you looked? Maybe he got tired and went to bed."

"Beth, yes or no? Is Peter there or not?" Jake
yelled.

Then Wally's voice in the background: "Jake,
they're home!"

And Jake hung up.

Five

▽

Search Party

Mr. Hatford came in the back door and put his car keys on the counter. Mother closed the door after them.

"Well, that was an interesting evening," she said. "The PTA is sponsoring a bake sale to buy caps and jerseys for the softball team next spring. I assume you boys are going to try out?"

Wally didn't answer. Neither did his brothers.

Mr. Hatford looked around. "My, aren't we quiet tonight! You guys get along okay while we were gone?"

"Sure. Why wouldn't we?" asked Josh, but his voice sounded funny, even to Wally.

Mother poured a glass of ice water from the refrigerator. "Peter in bed? Did he take a bath like I told him?"

Wally, Jake, and Josh looked at each other. "Uh, I'm not sure," Wally said.

Mother looked at him. "What do you mean, you're not sure? Did he run any bathwater or not?"

"I didn't hear any," Wally said miserably.

"Well, for heaven's sake. I specifically asked you boys to make sure Peter took a bath." Mother clunked her glass on the counter and started for the stairs.

"Uh . . . Mom," said Josh. "He's not there."

Mother turned around. "What do you mean, he's not there?"

And then it occurred to Wally that maybe he was! Maybe Peter had got tired of waiting for the boys and simply walked back home and went to bed all by himself. Of course! Why hadn't they thought of that!

"Maybe he *is*!" he said brightly.

Mrs. Hatford walked back into the kitchen. "Is he or *not*? *Where* is Peter?"

Jake had already run by her to check, but a moment later he came back down. "He's not there."

Now Mrs. Hatford sounded frantic. "Where *is* he?" She grabbed Wally by the shoulders. "Wallace Hatford, where is your brother?"

"We left him on a rock."

Mrs. Hatford gave a screech and Father took over. "Josh! Jake!" he commanded. "Get over here."

The boys lined up.

"What happened?"

Jake stuck his hands in his pants pockets and stared at the floor. "We were horsing around over by the Malloys', that's all. We left Peter on that big rock by their driveway, and when we got back a few minutes later he was gone. We were just going over there to—"

Mrs. Hatford sat down weakly in a chair. "Well, *call* them, for heaven's sake, and ask if they've seen him!"

"We already did."

"Then get over there immediately and *look* for him!" their father bellowed. "Don't you boys have a grain of sense in your heads? I'm going to get a flashlight and check out this side of the river; then I'll meet you across the bridge."

"If you find out *any*thing, call me," said Mother. "I'm going to stay right here by the phone. Boys, I can't *believe* you'd do something like this."

The boys spilled out onto the porch as fast as they could and broke into a run.

Wally didn't feel so good. What *had* happened to Peter? What if there *was* an abaguchie? How could a little seven-year-old kid be sitting there at the end of the driveway one minute but not the next? What if a kidnapper had come along and taken him, bunny slippers and all? He was surprised to find tears in his eyes.

The swinging bridge bounced briskly as their feet thudded across the wooden planks.

"Please let Peter be there, please let Peter be there," Wally whispered under his breath.

When they reached the other side, however, they stopped and looked at each other.

"Who's going to go up to the door and knock?" Josh said. "This was your idea, Jake. You've got to go."

"You were willing enough," said Jake. And then, to Wally, "You were the one who was carrying Peter on your back. You were the one who put him down on the rock in the first place. *You* ought to go."

This always happened. No matter how much Wally tried to stay out of trouble, he didn't.

"Oh, we'll all go," said Josh. "We were all in on it. We'll just walk up on their porch, ring the doorbell, and ask if Peter's there. Mr. and Mrs. Malloy ought to be home by now. They're not going to lie to us."

They started up the slope of the Malloys' driveway, and there, on the rock, sat Peter in his bunny slippers.

"Where *were* you?" asked the three boys together.

"Here," said Peter.

"What do you mean, *here*?" Jake demanded.

"Around," said Peter.

"You were *not*, Peter! We looked and looked for

you, and went all the way home and called the Malloys. Mom's worried to death," said Wally.

"I just went in their house for a root-beer float and came right out again," said Peter.

His brothers stared. "You just walked in there and asked for a root-beer float?" Wally asked incredulously.

"No. Eddie came and got me and asked did I want a root-beer float. I said yes."

Wally's shoulders slumped. So did Jake's and Josh's.

"Oh, no!" said Jake. "He spilled everything!"

"Why didn't you *tell* us where you were going?" Josh demanded.

"You weren't around."

"Well, you never should have left that rock," said Wally. "You can't just walk off like that."

"You walked off and left *me*!" Peter said.

"What did you *tell* the girls, anyway?" Josh demanded.

"*Nothing!* They already knew. They said you were playing wolf."

Jake let out a howl and clutched his head.

"See?" said Peter smugly.

"We're dead," said Wally. "We are cooked! Fried! All that running around looking scared was just an act. The girls are probably still laughing over it."

They walked glumly back toward the house, and
met their father on the bridge.

Mr. Hatford was very relieved to see Peter, and
Mother was so glad that she let him go to bed without his bath after all. But to the others she said,
"When you lose my trust, boys, you have to start
earning it all over again. And right now, I'm deeply
disappointed in you."

Hoo boy! thought Wally.

∇ • ∇ • ∇ • ∇ • ∇ • ∇ • ∇ • ∇ • ∇ • ∇ • ∇

Six

∇

Chiffon

"**Y**ou guys must have thought you were so smart, playing that tape of wolves howling and trying to make us think it was the abaguchie," Caroline said to Wally in school the next morning, poking him in the back with her pencil.

Wally turned around. "And *you* must have thought *you* were so smart to get Peter in your house so we'd have to look for him," Wally replied.

"Caroline, are you ready to listen?" Miss Applebaum said.

"Yes," Caroline told her, and the history lesson continued.

The boys didn't say much to the girls all week, nor the girls to the boys. Eddie said that when she went to the all-purpose room after school to shoot baskets, the boys jeered every time she missed, but didn't say anything at all when she made a basket, which was at least half the time.

Beth said that she and Josh were standing in line at the library to check out books, and Josh wouldn't even speak to her.

Caroline didn't care whether Wally ever spoke to her or not. Eddie's idea of bringing Peter into their kitchen while his brothers went crazy looking for him was one of the best tricks Eddie had pulled yet.

•

Saturday morning, as soon as the girls were up, Mother said, "I've baked another one of my pumpkin chiffon pies, and I want you to get it downtown to the bake sale by nine o'clock. I'll come by later and buy something for our own dinner."

"Do we all have to go?" whined Beth. "I'm reading *Mystery of the Haunted Shipwreck*, and it's so good, I can't put it down."

"You don't all have to go, but it might be nice if you asked the women if you could help," Mother said.

"Oh, let's all walk down," said Eddie. "It's for the softball team, after all. Maybe we'll make some points with the teachers."

They carried the pie carefully in the heavy cardboard box Mother had handed them. This time they walked to the end of Island Avenue, crossed the road bridge into the business district, and went up the block to City Hall.

"Look," said Beth, because there, going up the steps of City Hall, were the four Hatford brothers, carrying an even bigger box.

Caroline did not ask the boys if they were thinking about the time she threw their mother's chocolate chiffon cake in the river because she thought it was a trick. And the Hatfords certainly did not say anything to the girls about what they had done to Mrs. Malloy's pumpkin chiffon pie that the girls had delivered at their mother's instruction. Both mothers seemed to take to chiffon, that was certain.

Inside City Hall there was a large folding table spread with white paper. A big sign in the center said BUCKMAN ELEMENTARY PTA. There were trays of thick brownies, large platters of chocolate-chip cookies, lemon pies, angel food cakes—buttery squares of walnut fudge, and plates of coconut macaroons.

Evidently the Hatford boys, as well, had been told to see if they could help, because they hung around one end of the long table, the Malloy girls at the other.

"If you girls want to make yourselves useful, you could cut off squares of waxed paper so we'll have them ready when a customer orders," said the librarian, who seemed to be in charge.

And then to the boys, "Some of the customers want to eat their purchases right here. Could you make sure the cup dispenser is full over there by the coffeemaker, with plenty of cream and sugar? The supplies are under the table."

The Hatford boys set to work putting out cups and creamers.

More and more things were added to the table as mothers and fathers stopped in at City Hall. Customers came and went.

About ten-fifteen Mrs. Malloy walked in the front door and, not ten paces behind her, Mrs. Hatford.

"Why, hello, Ellen," Caroline's mother said. "Just look at all this! I hardly know what to choose."

"Well, the only thing I can vouch for is my chocolate chiffon cake," said Mrs. Hatford, pointing it out. "The same one I sent once to you."

Caroline gulped. She knew what was coming next.

Mother stared at the chocolate chiffon cake, then at Mrs. Hatford. "*You* sent us a cake?"

Now Mrs. Hatford was staring back. "I did indeed! The week after you moved in."

"Why, Ellen, I never got it!" Mother declared.

Caroline glanced over at the boys to see them listening in horror.

"That's impossible!" said Mrs. Hatford. "I sent my boys to deliver it themselves, and your girls returned the plate."

Mother looked at the chocolate chiffon cake, and then at Caroline, Beth, and Eddie. There was fire in her eyes, but with Mother, manners always took over temporarily.

"Well, since I never got it, the least I can do is try it now, Ellen, and I'm sure it's every bit as good as it looks," said Mother, and asked the librarian to wrap it up for her.

Mrs. Hatford was looking very puzzled.

"And if you want another of my pumpkin chiffon pies, I brought one again," Mother added. "My great-aunt Minna's recipe."

Mrs. Hatford gave a little smile and touched Mother's arm. "Jean, dear, you really shouldn't pretend to bake if you don't. Everyone in Buckman knows Ethel's pies. We all use that bakery."

"What?" cried Mother. "I never sent you a bakery pie. I baked a pumpkin chiffon pie myself." And she pointed it out on the table. "Didn't the pie I sent you look like that?"

Mrs. Hatford leaned down and studied the pie on the table. "No, indeed, it did not! The pie that came in your hatbox, Jean, was a pie from Ethel's Bakery."

Mother turned toward the girls.

"Caroline, have you any idea what happened to the chocolate chiffon cake that Mrs. Hatford baked for us?"

Caroline swallowed. "I—I threw it in the river," she said, her face burning.

"Threw it . . . in the . . . river?" Mrs. Hatford looked as though she were going to have a heart attack. But when she turned to ask her boys about the pumpkin chiffon pie, the boys weren't there. It was as though an abaguchie had swallowed them up.

Seven

▽

Confession

"**W**allace, Joseph, Joshua, and Peter!" yelled Mother, and she sounded like a drill sergeant.

She sounded like a drill sergeant who had just discovered that someone had made off with a pumpkin chiffon pie. A pumpkin chiffon pie made by somebody's own hands from a recipe of someone's great-aunt Minna.

The boys moved reluctantly into the hall from the living room and stood with feet poised as though ready to run the other way.

"What," said Mrs. Hatford slowly, taking off her sweater, "happened to a certain pumpkin chiffon pie baked by Mrs. Malloy and delivered to our very door a month ago?"

Peter looked at Wally, Wally at Josh, Josh at Jake, and Jake looked down at his knees. "We ate it," he said.

"Ate it? *All* of it? The four of you?"

The boys nodded, all four of them.

"Why? Why didn't you save any for dinner? Why did you go out and buy a pie from Ethel's Bakery, and try to make me think that was the pie Mrs. Malloy sent? I even thanked her for a bakery pie! I've never been so embarrassed in my life." She looked sternly at the boys. "Jake? . . . Josh? . . . Wally . . . ?"

Wally couldn't stand it any longer. "We destroyed it," he said.

Mother continued to stare. "I can't believe this."

"We were looking for dog doo," added Peter.

"What?" cried Mother. "Have you boys gone stark raving mad?"

"We thought the girls might have baked the pie and put something awful in it," muttered Josh.

"Why would those three sweet girls do something like that?"

"Easy," cried Jake. "Very easy. I could see the Malloy girls doing about anything you could think of."

"Sweet? Ha!" said Josh.

"Remember," Wally reminded her, "they threw your cake in the river."

Mrs. Hatford shook her head. "That I don't understand at all. *Some*thing must have happened to make them do that. What did they think was possibly inside that box?"

"Dead birds," said Peter.

"What?"

"Ellen, quit while you're ahead," Mr. Hatford said from the dining room, gobbling down his lunch before he delivered the afternoon mail. "The more you ask, the more they'll tell you, and the more you find out, the more upset you're going to be."

So Wally and his brothers escaped upstairs. Mrs. Hatford went out on the back porch to cool off, and Mr. Hatford finished his Saturday-afternoon rounds.

When the paper came out that evening, however, the chocolate chiffon cake and the pumpkin chiffon pie were forgotten temporarily, because there was something on page two of the front section that interested them all:

ABAGUCHIE AGAIN?

Another sighting of the elusive abaguchie was reported yesterday by a man in the Stonecoal area of Upshur County.

Clyde M. Downs and his wife, Marlene, were sitting down to dinner when a low growling by their springer spaniel sent them outside to investigate.

Marlene Downs saw a large animal run out of the yard with a chicken in its mouth. At first glance, she recounted, it seemed to her a cougar, but in other ways it resembled a wolf. Clyde Downs thought it to be a member of the cat family, but like no cat he had seen before.

Police report that the paw prints and bits of fur recovered from the scene were inconclusive. . . .

"What do you think this means?" Mrs. Hatford asked her husband at dinner.

"I think somebody's large dog is loose, and an awful lot of folks are letting their imaginations run away with them," said Mr. Hatford.

"If there *is* a creature like that running around, Tom, we ought to be awfully careful about leaving our doors and windows unlocked," said Mother.

"Ellen, if there is a creature like that around Buckman, it's a *creature*, not a human," said her husband. "It's not as though it's going around opening windows."

Wally lay in bed that night and wondered what he would do if *he* were to see the abaguchie. Write the Bensons down in Georgia, he decided. Maybe *that* would bring them back.

▽ • ▽ • ▽ • ▽ • ▽ • ▽ • ▽ • ▽ • ▽ • ▽ • ▽

Eight

▽

Eddie's Thumb

Eddie found the story when she was looking up football scores the next day. Caroline had only half believed Wally Hatford's story about the abaguchie, but if a *newspaper* printed a story like that, it was true, wasn't it?

They talked about it at breakfast.

"Did you see this?" Eddie asked, showing the story to her father.

"Clyde Downs and his wife wouldn't lie, would they?" asked Beth.

"Remember that when you're frightened, you can think you saw things that weren't really there," Mother said.

Father agreed. "You might see a mountain lion up in the hills, but around here it would be pretty unusual."

Caroline looked about her warily. "I thought it

45

was just some animal people saw out in the woods. I didn't know it actually came in people's yards."

Beth's eyes were as big as fried eggs. "Think what a wonderful book that would make," she breathed. *"The Age of the Abaguchie; The Abaguchie Stalks; The Abaguchie's Revenge . . ."*

But Caroline was not interested in books about abaguchies. She wondered what it would be like to be an actress in such a movie. Just suppose she was this young girl in this big house all by herself, and it's getting dark outside, and she's forgotten to lock the doors. Maybe she's reading a book, and she hears a noise on the front porch.

She puts down the book and waits and listens. And finally she realizes she hasn't locked the side door. So she gets up in the darkened room and goes to the side door. She puts both hands up to her eyes and peers through the glass. And there, right on the other side of the glass, only inches away, are two red eyes, staring right back at her.

Caroline wrapped her arms around herself and shivered. She imagined being given that role in a movie—how she would clutch her throat and scream.

Or perhaps she realized she hadn't locked the side door, and just as she got to it, it swung wide open, and there was this horrible creature, and . . .

Or maybe she would get up and go lock the door,

but meanwhile, unknown to her, the abaguchie had crept around and come in the back, so that when she was locking the side door, the abaguchie crept up behind her, grabbed her by the throat, and . . .

Caroline made gurgling, choking sounds.

"Are you all right, Caroline?" asked her father. "Drink a little juice."

"I was attacked," said Caroline, breathing heavily.

"By what?" asked Mother.

"An abaguchie came in and grabbed me by the throat."

"Oh, for goodness' sake, Caroline!" said Mother.

"I just wanted to know what it would feel like if one *did* get in the house, and *did* creep up behind me, and *did* put its claws around my neck," Caroline said.

"If that happened, my dear, you would not make another sound for the rest of your life," said her father. "If you would like to practice not making another sound for the rest of the morning, I wouldn't mind at all."

•

The afternoon was overcast and chilly, but Eddie talked Beth and Caroline into going to the field behind the college to practice her batting and pitching. It wasn't Caroline's favorite way to spend a Sunday, and Beth had her nose in a book all the way there, but when one of the sisters needed something, the others usually came through.

"What I need," Eddie told them, "is for someone to pitch to me, and the other to stand in the outfield. After that I need to practice my pitching."

"Whatever," said Beth, and almost stepped off the bank of the river. Caroline had to guide her onto the swinging bridge and make sure she got off the other end all right.

There wasn't anyone else at the field, so Caroline took her place in the outfield with Dad's old glove, while Beth pitched.

Eddie *was* good, Caroline could tell. She would have been even better if Beth were a better pitcher, but more times than not she cracked the ball so hard that Caroline was convinced it was going right across the river.

Whap!

Whop!

And then the ball was soaring high up in the air, while Eddie gave a whoop and made a run around the ball diamond.

"They've *got* to let you on the softball team, Eddie!" Caroline told her when they took a break. "You're better than some of the boys we see practicing after school. You're better than Jake Hatford!"

Eddie herself looked determined. "I'm going to

practice my guts out between now and March, just in case," she said.

She became pitcher next, and Beth and Caroline took turns batting the ball, just so Eddie could practice getting it over the plate. Pitching a curveball, a fastball, lifting her left foot and drawing her arm far back.

"All you need to do now is spit," Beth laughed.

Whack! Beth hit the ball straight out this time toward Eddie, and as Eddie reached up to catch it, it hit her thumb, bending it backward.

"Ow!" Eddie howled in pain, holding her wrist with the other hand.

"Oh, Eddie, I'm sorry!" Beth cried, dropping the bat and running over.

Now Eddie had both hands between her knees. She was bent over with her eyes scrunched up.

"Oh, my hand!" she said, sucking in her breath.

"I'm sorry! I'm sorry!" Beth said again, looking miserable.

"It's not your fault," Eddie said. "I just hope my thumb's not broken."

"We'd better go home and let Dad look at it," Caroline said. "Maybe he'll put a splint on it or something." She picked up the ball and glove, Beth got her book, and they started home.

They had just reached the bridge when they saw the Hatford boys standing out in the road, throwing walnuts at trees along the river. When the boys saw the girls—specifically Eddie, wincing in pain—they stopped and stared.

"What happened?" called Josh.

"Don't tell them," Eddie whispered through clenched teeth.

But someone had to tell them something—you couldn't just say nothing, when anyone could plainly see that Eddie was hurt, Caroline thought.

It was Beth who got the idea, however.

"She got bitten," Beth said, her face somber.

"By what?" yelled Jake. "A little bitty bug?"

Eddie had started across the bridge, but Beth faced the boys. "We're not sure," she said, her eyes fearful. "She went back into the bushes after a ball, and there was something there—some creature. It growled and bit her hand, but we never did see it."

Beth followed Eddie across the bridge and Caroline came last, but turned in time to see Jake and Josh and Wally and Peter staring at each other in horror.

Nine

▽

Tall Tale

Wally was prepared not to speak to the Malloy girls for the rest of his life, if necessary, if it would keep him from getting into any more trouble than he had. Mom was already upset with him and Jake and Josh because of the pie business, and then, when they told their dad that Eddie had got bitten by something, Mr. Hatford called the Malloys to find out what, and Coach Malloy told them it was just a sprained thumb.

So when he got to school on Monday, Wally took his seat without turning around, got out the spelling list he'd been working on over the weekend, and went right to work memorizing *bargain*, *separate*, *juicy*, and *argument*.

He was very surprised, therefore, when Caroline Malloy tapped him on the shoulder. He only half turned.

"What do you want?" he asked.

"I was just wondering," Caroline said, "if anyone ever found any bones."

"What?"

"If anyone ever found a skeleton of an abaguchie. I mean, if anyone did, couldn't scientists study it and find out what kind of an animal it is?"

Wally could hardly believe his ears. Caroline was asking *him*? Caroline was going to believe whatever *he* told her? His mind whirred. Over in the corner Miss Applebaum was pinning up a list of class helpers for the week—who had lunchroom cleanup, who had blackboard cleanup, who took the volleyballs out to the playground at recess, and so on.

He turned around a little more.

"Well, he doesn't want anyone to know," Wally said.

"Who doesn't?"

"Mr. Oldaker."

"Who's that?"

"The man who owns the bookstore. Nobody's supposed to know about the bones, and if I told you, you'd just tell your sisters."

"I would not."

"Ha!" said Wally, and turned forward again. "Sure, you wouldn't!"

Nothing happened for a moment or two, and then there was another tap on Wally's shoulder.

"*What?*" Wally said, acting annoyed. This time he turned around far enough to see Caroline's face. Her eyes were wide and she had a sort of earnest look that he would have liked on a girl if it wasn't on the face of a Malloy.

"*Tell* me, Wally," Caroline begged, and her voice was gentle, pleading.

"You're nuts!"

"*Please!*"

"You'd blab the minute you got out of school, and Mr. Oldaker would really be mad, because the only other person in town who's supposed to know is my dad, which is the only reason *I* know."

"Well, if only your father is supposed to know and now *you* know, *he* must have blabbed," said Caroline.

Wally faced the front of the room again. When he and Caroline were not speaking, she drove him nuts. When he and Caroline *were* speaking, she drove him nuts. It was hopeless. He couldn't escape. His destiny was to be driven absolutely crazy by Caroline Malloy.

The notes of "The Star Spangled Banner" sounded over the loudspeaker, and Wally slid from his seat with his hand over his heart and stood at attention until Miss Applebaum said they could sit. Then the teacher started the spelling test.

At least he had until recess to think about what to

say next, Wally was thinking. Now that he'd told Caroline there was some big secret about the abaguchie, he had to figure out what it was. His mouth had run on faster than his brain could keep up. Why had he brought in Mr. Oldaker? Why, the minute Caroline had asked about bones, had he thought of the bookstore?

The only reason Wally could think of was that there was a trapdoor in the very center of the floor of Oldakers'. Because it led to an old storage cellar, and because the floor of the cellar was dirt, it seemed to Wally a perfect place to bury treasure. Treasure or a dead body or both. And because he had once helped Mr. Oldaker bring up some boxes from the cellar, and because Caroline had asked about bones, that was probably why he had thought of Mr. Oldaker's cellar.

When the bell rang for recess, Miss Applebaum was first out the door to take her attendance sheet to the office, and the others followed her in a line because they were going to divide up into teams and play kickball.

Wally loved kickball, and he was hurrying so fast to get out of the room that he jerked too hard on the jacket he had stuffed in his desktop and pulled out a box of sixty-four crayons, spilling them all across the floor.

"Rats!" Wally yelled, furious at himself. Not only did he want to make sure he was on the first team for kickball but he wanted to get away from Caroline the Crazy as well.

He stopped to pick up every crayon, some of which had rolled as far as two rows away. When he got them all into the box at last, and turned to go out the door, he found Caroline blocking the doorway— her hands and feet braced tightly against the sides, her feet six inches off the floor.

"*Move* it!" said Wally.

Caroline didn't budge. "I'm not moving till you tell me the secret of the bones," she said.

"What?"

"The secret Mr. Oldaker told your father about the abaguchie," Caroline insisted.

Wally's first thought was to push her out of the way, but she was wedged tightly there in the door frame, arms and legs spread like a big X. It would take more than a little push to loosen her, and if he gave a *big* push, she'd go sprawling into the hallway, and then he would be in big trouble.

"What did Mr. Oldaker tell your dad, Wally? *Tell* me!" Caroline insisted.

There wasn't anything left to do. Wally lowered his voice. "Promise you won't tell."

"Promise."

Wally's mind was like a runaway truck barreling down a steep hill without any brakes. "A couple of years ago," he lied, "they were digging out more of Oldaker's cellar beneath his store, and somebody found bones."

He watched Caroline's feet slide down both sides of the door frame until she landed with a plop on the soles of her sneakers.

Wally's mind raced on and on. He was a better storyteller than he'd thought. Tall tales, that's what he was telling. How could you call something this wild a lie? If Caroline believed him, that was her problem.

"Whose *were* they?" Caroline breathed.

"Well . . . Dad says they weren't bones of any known animal. Mr. Oldaker thinks it could be the skeleton of an abaguchie, but they don't want people getting upset or staying away from the bookstore or anything, so they just haven't told anyone but Dad. As far as I know, the bones are still there."

Once again he tried to push past Caroline, and once again she braced her hands and feet against the sides. "Just tell me one more thing, Wally. How do I get in Oldakers' cellar?"

"There's a trapdoor beyond the cashier's counter. But they'd see you if you tried to go down there.

Take my word for it, Caroline, and don't try it. Now, *move!*"

Caroline moved. "Thank you very much, Wally," she called after him as he ran headlong out to the playground. Finally, he was free.

Ten

▽

The Secret Staircase

If Caroline had ever considered skipping school, this was the time. It would have been so easy to just walk to the edge of the school yard and keep going. She could tell Beth and Eddie about it later.

But the more she thought about it, the more she realized that one of two things could happen, and probably both:

1. Miss Applebaum would realize she was missing and would call home.

2. Mr. Oldaker would wonder why she wasn't in school and might even phone the school office. She had to wait.

She had promised Wally she wouldn't tell her sisters, but her shoelaces were crossed when she said it, and *everybody* knows that if something is crossed when you promise, it isn't a promise at all.

At lunchtime she sought out Beth and Eddie and told them what she had learned from Wally.

"Let's go to the bookstore today!" she said. "Two of us can be lookouts, and the other can climb through the trapdoor."

She hoped Eddie would say that she, Caroline, could be the one to go down.

"We'll do it, but not this afternoon," said Eddie. "I've got to write a report on Balboa."

"I'm not going anywhere until I finish this book," said Beth. "Caroline, you should read it! *Land of the Leeches*! It will make your skin crawl!"

Caroline's heart sank. "How many more chapters?" she asked.

"I just started. Sixteen, I think."

Caroline was dismayed. She couldn't count on her sisters. Hadn't she spent a whole hour Sunday afternoon batting balls just so Eddie could practice her pitching? Now, when *she* needed a little help, where were Beth and Eddie?

In the next thirty seconds Caroline decided two things:

1. She could not stand knowing that the trapdoor was there in the bookstore and she couldn't go through it today.

2. She would do it alone, and not tell anyone about it till it was over.

Her mind raced on ahead of her. *The Secret Stair-*

case, starring Caroline Lenore Malloy. What a wonderful movie that would make! In fact, getting ready for the part was almost as much fun as doing it.

First, the costume. Dark. No, not dark. Mousy. Sort of brownish-grayish. Something to blend in with the woodwork. Nothing too light or too dark, too loud or too dramatic. A pair of faded jeans, an old jacket that Beth had given her, worn-out sneakers—that should do it.

What should she take? A flashlight to look for the bones once she got down there; a screwdriver, in case the trapdoor was screwed shut.

The bell rang and Caroline dreamily took her seat again behind Wally, hardly even noticing him. When an actress has been given a role, she in turn gives her heart to her performance, Caroline knew. A role like this required a full range of acting ability:

Cautious excitement: Caroline wrote it down on the back of her spelling paper. She would leave to begin the adventure like Joan of Arc, going off into battle, confident that she could discover the abaguchie's bones.

Deep foreboding: That was what her face would have to show next. Caroline wrote that down too. She imagined that Wally's back was a mirror and she was studying her own face in it. The forehead would be frowning. The teeth would be set—clenched, perhaps. Eyes narrowed, thinking.

And then, of course, when she reached the bottom of the secret staircase and discovered she was in the abaguchie's lair, there would be sudden terror!

Caroline bolted back in her seat, making her eyes wild. Huge! Her lips would be slightly parted. Her throat would feel—

"Caroline Malloy, do you want to see the nurse?" came Miss Applebaum's voice.

Caroline blinked. Where was she? What was she doing here in this classroom? Where was the secret staircase?

"Do you have a pain somewhere?" the teacher asked.

"No."

"You looked as though you might be having an attack of some sort."

The other children giggled. Wally's shoulders were shaking with laughter, but Caroline didn't even care.

"Do you think you might be able to take part in our geography discussion?" the teacher asked. "We were discussing petroleum products, Caroline. Can you tell us where in the world we might find the most oil?"

"At the bottom of the secret staircase," said Caroline dreamily.

Eleven

▽

Waiting for Caroline

"I think," said Wally, on the way home from school with his brothers that afternoon, "that the spider is about to capture the fly."

"What spider?" asked Peter, skipping to keep up with his older brothers.

Wally, Jake, and Josh exchanged looks.

"What *fly*?" Peter demanded.

"What I mean is, we're about to trap Caroline," Wally told him.

"Don't tell Peter!" Josh said. "He'll blab."

"I *won't*!"

"You won't on purpose, Peter, but sometimes you let things slip," Jake told him.

"I won't!" Peter screeched, stopping there on the sidewalk, fists clenched, eyes scrunched up in fury.

"Okay, but not *one* word to anybody!" Wally warned. "I'll bet my last nickel that as soon as school is out, Caroline is going to Oldakers' bookstore and go down in that cellar when no one's looking."

"Why?" asked Jake.

"Because she asked me about the abaguchie today. She said if there *were* abaguchies around Buckman, somebody should have found some bones. And then it came to me—this idea, sort of." He grinned just a little.

"Well?" said Jake.

"I told her there *were* some bones—that nobody knew what they belonged to—and that they were down in the cellar of Oldakers' bookstore. I just know she's going to go there today and sneak down in that cellar."

"So?" said Jake.

"Then what?" asked Josh.

So? Then what? After all his brilliant work luring Caroline to the cellar, his brothers didn't know what to do?

"What do you mean, then what?" squawked Wally. And he suddenly realized he didn't know either. He put his imagination on fast-forward. "Then we'll—we'll all go in and stand on top of the trapdoor so she can't get out."

"That's *it*!" said Jake. "That's perfect! You're a genius, Wally."

But Peter looked worried. "Not *ever*?"

"Don't be stupid, Peter. Of course we'll let her out sometime. Just not right away, that's all," Josh told him.

"So we can't let her out of sight for a minute," said Wally. He pointed. "There she is, going over the bridge with her sisters. Maybe they'll *all* go down into Oldakers' cellar."

"If they see us following them, though, they won't," warned Jake. "What we've got to do is go stand inside the drugstore where we can watch the door of Oldakers'."

"And, Peter, if you blab, you can't come with us," Josh told him.

"I *won't* blab! I just think we ought to put some food down there or something."

"Food?" said Wally.

"In case they get hungry."

"Peter, we're talking about fifteen or twenty minutes. Anybody can go without food for fifteen or twenty minutes."

Peter looked much relieved. "Okay, then," he said.

As soon as the boys put their schoolbooks on the table and grabbed a handful of cheese crackers, they were off again, heading toward the business district. A quick glance inside Oldakers' told them the girls weren't there yet, so they crowded into Larkin's Pharmacy and went over to the window.

Mr. Larkin, the pharmacist, looked up from his pills and bottles. "How ya doin', boys?"

"Okay," said Wally.

They took positions just far enough back so they couldn't be easily seen, but close enough to the window so that Caroline and her sisters could not get into the bookstore unnoticed.

Four o'clock became four-thirty. The cashier glanced over at them. "Anything I can do for you?" she asked.

"Uh . . . no, thanks," said Wally.

"I'll bet she doesn't come," Jake whispered. "Maybe she had a piano lesson or something."

"Yeah, who says that even if she comes, it'll be today?" said Josh.

Wally was getting a little peeved. "Well, just go on home, then," he said hotly. "Just go on home and miss her if she *does* come. Oldakers' closes at six. If she's not here by then, we'll leave."

"What are we supposed to tell Mr. Larkin?" whispered Jake. "He keeps looking over at us. So does the cashier."

Wally looked around. The magazines were at the back of the store beside the prescription counter. The games were over by the soda fountain along one wall, one of the last soda fountains left in the state of West Virginia. Up here beneath the front window was a rack of women's socks and underwear. To his left was a shelf of Ace bandages.

Mr. Larkin was walking toward the front of the store.

"You boys waiting for somebody?" he asked.

"No, uh . . . we're trying to decide what to buy," Wally said, because neither Jake nor Josh said a word, and Peter had wandered off to look for Matchbox cars on the toy rack.

"Maybe I can help," said the pharmacist.

Wally desperately focused on the women's socks and underwear, and just as quickly turned his attention to the Ace bandages.

"I was sort of looking for a knee bandage," he said.

"An elastic knee sleeve? For yourself? Well, let's measure you and see," Mr. Larkin said.

Wally exchanged horrified looks with Josh and Jake. He didn't have any money with him, and even if he had, he wouldn't spend it on an elastic knee sleeve.

"It's—it's not for me, it's for my dad," he said quickly. And then, because he knew Mr. Larkin would wonder why Dad wasn't buying it himself, said, "He hurt his knee so bad, he can hardly walk."

"I'm sorry to hear that," Mr. Larkin said. "Why don't I call home and ask him to measure around his knee, and—"

At that precise moment Wally saw Caroline Malloy walking along the other side of the street toward Oldakers', carrying a flashlight!

"I'll be right back, Mr. Larkin," he said. "I'll go home and measure Dad's knee myself."

And as soon as Caroline went inside the bookstore, the boys crossed the street and watched furtively through Oldakers' store window.

Twelve

▽

Trapped

Caroline's idea had been to go right home from school, check in with Mother, grab a doughnut or something, and then, when Beth and Eddie were settling down to their homework, slip out of the house with Mother's flashlight and Dad's screwdriver, and go to Oldakers' by herself.

Now, however, everything seemed to conspire to keep her from getting outside of the house. Mother told her that before she did anything else, she was to clean her room, change the linen on her bed, and put her dirty sheets in the hamper.

Caroline had done this as quickly as she could, but it took a long time, and before she could leave her room, even, Mother came up to check. She said Caroline had to go through the clothes in her closet as well, and sort out clean from dirty.

And then, when she had finally found the flashlight and screwdriver and was on her way to the front door, a friend called from school and wanted to talk about the *stupidest* things—paper dolls of all the country singers, for heaven's sake.

Out the door at last. Down the steps. It was really getting cold now in Buckman, and she was glad she had thought to put on Beth's old jacket with the fur trim.

The sky was already gray, and Caroline was glad to see, as she crossed the large road bridge at the end of Island Avenue and headed toward Main Street, that the Hatford boys were nowhere in sight. If this was a trick, and there wasn't any trapdoor at Oldakers', she didn't want Wally laughing at her. If he and his brothers were in the store, she'd buy a book—any book—and pretend that's what she'd come for in the first place.

When she got to the store, she slipped the flashlight and screwdriver up one sleeve of her jacket and went inside, glad to get out of the chill. When the sun went down in West Virginia, it went in a hurry, as though there were just day and night, with not much evening in between.

It didn't take long to find the trapdoor. If you had been coming to Oldakers' Bookstore for years and years you probably wouldn't even notice it anymore, but Caroline's eyes sought it out, and there it was, not too far from the cashier's counter.

There were customers ambling about, so Caroline strolled casually toward the back. The store was warm and welcoming, and she wondered why she hadn't been here before. She couldn't believe the large collection of children's books. It reminded her of the school library. There were books that made her laugh, like *Howling for Home*. There was a large tent for younger children, with many of the favorite picture books she had enjoyed when she was little— *Frog and Toad Are Friends* and *When the Relatives Came*.

As soon as the space around the trapdoor was empty, Caroline walked over to see if the lid was screwed or bolted down. Wonder of wonders, there was nothing holding it at all. It was just sitting there, over the opening. Her heart began to race.

Was it possible that, for once in his life, Wally Hatford had been telling her the truth?

Now the problem was how to get through the trapdoor without anyone seeing. Customers called two different men "Mr. Oldaker," so Caroline figured the owners were a young man and his father.

Since it was almost dinnertime, there were only a few customers in the store, and some of them were leaving. This could be her lucky day, Caroline thought. She hung around, moving slowly among the racks of new calendars, of notepaper and stationery, past the shelves of paperback books and dictionaries and large flat books with beautiful pictures that people kept on their coffee tables back in Ohio.

"Well, Mike, I'm going to head home," she heard the older Mr. Oldaker say to the other. "I'll set up that sale table, and there will be time tomorrow morning to put the merchandise on it."

"Okay, then. I'll leave at six," the younger man said, and after a little more talk with a woman who came in just then, the older man left.

"Do you have any books with photographs about the way Chinese children live?" the woman asked Mike Oldaker.

"Have you seen *City Kids in China*?" he suggested, and led her to the back of the store.

Caroline looked around. No one else was there.

She moved quickly over to the trapdoor and bent down, grasping the edge with her fingers. At first it didn't seem to move, and she was afraid it might be nailed shut after all, but was relieved to find she could lift it with both hands. She slid it off to one side.

Caroline could see narrow, steep stairs just inside. Before she could think of any reason she should not go, she started down, pulling the lid back over her as she moved down the stairs until she felt it settle into place above her head.

She stood very still, heart pounding, the damp,

musty smell of earth filling her nostrils, the cold of the ground seeping into her bones.

This is what it's like to be buried alive! she thought. *Buried Alive*, starring Caroline Lenore Malloy.

Any minute she expected the trapdoor above her to open and Mike Oldaker to stare down at her. But as she waited, the sound of footsteps grew louder from the back of the store, and passed right over her head. No one lifted the door.

Emboldened at last by the talk and laughter, the comings and goings above her head, Caroline turned on the flashlight and directed it to the bottom of the steep, narrow steps as she went on down.

There were cobwebs everywhere. Goose bumps rose on her arms. She was the daughter of a kind king but had an evil stepmother. And while her father was out of the country, the stepmother had her put in a dungeon, hoping she would die before her father returned.

At this point, Caroline knew, a sob should escape her lips. The books always said so, and Caroline practiced it, giving out soft little sobs that would not be heard from above, just tiny baby sobs as she moved on around the cellar, brushing cobwebs away from her face.

There were a few boxes on the dirt floor of the cellar, some wooden window frames standing on end, assorted junk, but mostly the place seemed unused. Any books stored here for long would become damp and moldy, Caroline was sure.

She started in one corner, working her way along, moving a box here, a crate there. The cellar wasn't as large as the floor above, so it did not take long for her to cover every foot of space with the beam of her flashlight. She was looking for bones—a piece of a skeleton sticking up out of the floor, perhaps. Something hidden that only Mr. Hatford and the Oldakers knew about. There was nothing. Absolutely nothing.

Could they have dug up the bones and taken them somewhere else? Thrown them away? She began looking in all the boxes, but the boxes were empty.

What a disappointment! Well, Wally didn't have to know she'd come. If he ever told her again about the bones in the cellar of Oldakers', she'd just say, "Ha!" and not listen. But right now she was cold, and Mother was having chicken and dumplings for supper, her favorite. So Caroline went back to the stairs again, climbed up just far enough so that her hands would reach the trapdoor.

This would be the hard part. It was a lot easier getting *into* the cellar unseen than it would be getting *out*. She waited until the footsteps and voices went to the back of the store again. When she felt quite sure that no one was up there by the trapdoor, she put both hands against it and shoved. Nothing happened.

She frowned. Caroline turned on the flashlight to be sure it was the door she was pushing against. Then she turned off the light once more, stuck it again up the sleeve of her jacket, and braced the palms of her hands against the underside of the trap door. Caroline pushed with all her strength.

The door didn't budge. There must be a customer standing right there on top.

Thirteen

▽

Alarm

The boys took turns standing on it, two at a time, keeping as quiet as they could. Wally could feel the trapdoor moving slightly against the soles of his shoes. Any minute now Caroline would freak out. Any moment there would be a scream from under the floor and he and his brothers would look down as though they couldn't imagine where the sound was coming from.

Then Mike Oldaker would come over and lift the trapdoor, and Caroline would have to climb out, her face as red as Santa Claus's. And she'd have to explain that she was looking for abaguchie bones, and make a fool of herself, as usual.

Peter was at the back of the store, happily looking at picture books in the big indoor tent, and Wally was trying to pretend he was browsing. Women's socks and underwear in Larkin's, and now greeting cards at Oldakers'. It was the only thing he was close to from where he stood on the trapdoor.

"Help you fellas?" Mike Oldaker asked, restocking a stationery shelf nearby.

"Just looking for a card for—for my dad," Wally said quickly.

"Tom's sick, is he?"

"Hurt his knee," Wally continued, one lie piling on top of another. "Thought maybe you had something funny."

"The humorous cards are on the other side," Mr. Oldaker said. "I'm going to close, now, in about five minutes."

"*I'll* take a look at them," said Josh, and went around the rack.

With Josh gone Wally could really feel the trapdoor quiver beneath his feet and he expected a yell from Caroline. There was no sound from below, however, and he was disappointed. He wanted to be here when she came out.

"Six o'clock, boys. Store's closing," Mike Oldaker called.

"Come on, Peter, we're going home. Maybe I'll just make Dad a card myself," Josh told the owner.

Peter came sauntering to the door, running his finger along the display shelf, humming to himself, and at last the four boys said good-night and went out.

Peter stopped. "Hey! What about—?"

Wally clapped one hand over his mouth.

"Did she come out?" Peter whispered, wriggling free.

"No. She will when we're gone, though. Man, wouldn't you like to see her face when Oldaker sees her crawl up out of the cellar?"

They wanted to stay at the window and watch, but Mike Oldaker was looking at them, and besides, they'd be late for dinner as it was.

•

At home, as expected, Mother had dinner on the table. "Now, you *know* when we sit down to eat," she said to all four. "If I can go to the trouble to get food on the table, you can go to the wee bit of trouble it takes to get here on time."

Wally slid into his chair and stuffed a piece of bread in his mouth to show he was eating, and the meal began.

"Got the strangest call about a half hour ago," Mr. Hatford said, passing the pork chops. "Mr. Larkin called and asked how my knee was doing. Said he could drop off an elastic sleeve for it on his way home if I'd just give him the measurements. I told him he must have the wrong knee, 'cause mine were fine, and he said he guessed he'd misunderstood. Now, who do you suppose goes around talking about my knees?"

Mother burst into laughter. "Must be those shorts you wear in the summertime with your uniform, Tom. People see those knees of yours and figure they need all the help they can get."

Whew! Wally swallowed again, and this time there wasn't even any food in his mouth.

The phone rang again, and Mrs. Hatford got up, looking annoyed.

"Those people who call during the dinner hour!" she muttered. "If it's a salesman, Tom, I swear I'm going to hang up on him." She picked up the telephone on the wall. "Yes?"

Wally ate his potatoes next, and expected to hear the slam of the receiver as Mother hung up. Instead, he heard her voice saying, "Why, I'm not sure, Eddie. Let me check."

Mrs. Hatford turned to the others at the table. "It's Eddie Malloy, and she wants to know whether any of us have seen Caroline. She specifically asked if you had, Wally. Evidently she left without saying where she was going, and Eddie thought you might know where she is. They're worried."

Wally's mouth dropped open. Hadn't Caroline crawled out yet? Maybe she fell backward down the steps and had a brain concussion. Maybe she figured she was buried alive, and died of fright. Maybe there really *was* an abaguchie down there, and—

"Wally? Have you seen her?"

"At—at school," said Wally.

"And you haven't seen her since?"

"Maybe I did see her downtown, walking along Main Street." Wally turned to his brothers. "Did we see Caroline on Main Street?"

"Yeah, I think that was her walking toward Oldakers'."

Mother glanced over at Peter, who was sitting with his lips pressed tightly together, staring down at the table.

"Did *you* see her, Peter?"

He shook his head, lips pressed even tighter.

"You didn't see Caroline Malloy at all?"

"If they saw her, I saw her," Peter said.

Mother let out her breath. "There are times I think I have the strangest children in West Virginia," she told them, and then, into the receiver, "They seem to think they *might* have seen Caroline on Main Street near Oldakers'."

Just then there came the sound of Police Chief Decker's squad car, the siren getting louder and higher, then falling, then louder and higher again.

Tom Hatford, in addition to being one of Buckman's postmen, was also one of the sheriff's deputies. He got up from the table so fast that his chair tipped over backward, and ran outside to his car.

Fourteen

▽

Escape

As soon as Caroline heard the boys' voices on the floor above, she knew what had happened. Wally had made up that story of abaguchie bones being found in the cellar of Oldakers' bookstore because he knew she would go right down there to see. And she had trotted down Main Street, flashlight in hand, and now felt quite sure that the boys must have been watching for her from somewhere, laughing their heads off.

She stopped trying to push open the trapdoor. They must all be standing on it together. She listened.

"I'm going to close, now, in about five minutes," came Mike Oldaker's voice.

Ha! What would the boys do then? As soon as Mr. Oldaker sent them out the door, she would push open the trapdoor and . . .

She imagined the look on Mr. Oldaker's face as she rose up out of the floor. What would she *tell* him?

Caroline thought hard. She could say that—say that the boys had kidnapped her and thrown her in the cellar. That's it! She would crawl up through the trapdoor sort of . . . well, clawing at the air, as though she could hardly breathe. Then she would collapse on the floor right in front of Mike Oldaker, and—

The idea came to a sudden halt when she realized she would be caught with a screwdriver and flashlight in hand. She could always leave them behind, of course, but then how would she get them again?

Also, if she told a flat-out lie about the boys, Mr. Oldaker would probably call Mr. and Mrs. Hatford, and then *she'd* be in trouble.

She wasn't sure how long it was after the boys left that she heard Mike Oldaker emptying the cash register. Then there was the sound of the front door opening, closing again, and the key turning in the lock. Silence. *Now!*

Then a new thought occurred to her. What if she was locked in? What if she couldn't even open the door from the inside? Maybe she *should* have climbed out while Mr. Oldaker was still there.

"Help!" she cried suddenly, pushing her full weight against the trapdoor above her.

The door opened into darkness. There wasn't even a light on by the cash register. Caroline did not want to use her flashlight if she could help it for fear someone outside the store would see the light and think a robber was there. She carefully closed the trap again once she was out so she wouldn't fall into it in the darkness, and groped her way to the front door.

Locked. Oh, no! She tried again. Dead-bolt locked. Double-triple locked. Her heart began to pound. She really would catch it if Dad found out she'd hidden in the store past closing time. Already her parents were probably wondering where she was.

She made her way over to the counter and managed to knock a stapler to the floor before she found the telephone. Caroline dialed home, wishing with all her heart that one of her sisters would answer.

She was in luck.

"Hello?" said Beth.

"Beth, listen," Caroline said. "I've done something really stupid. I climbed down that trapdoor at Oldakers'."

"What?" Beth gasped. "Where are you?"

"The bookstore. Everyone's gone home."

"What was it like? What was down there?" Beth wanted a full description, Caroline realized, and all *she* wanted was to go home.

"Nothing. Absolutely nothing. The boys must have

been watching, and waited till I went down, and then stood on the trapdoor so I couldn't crawl back out. I heard their voices. I waited till they left and Mr. Oldaker locked up, but now I can't get the front door open. What am I going to do?"

"Have you tried the back door? Almost every store has a back door," Beth suggested.

"Okay, I'll try, but listen. Make some excuse for me, and if I'm not there in fifteen minutes, you'll have to call Mr. Oldaker to come and let me out. Are you having dinner?"

"It's almost ready. Wait a minute, Caroline. Here's Eddie."

Caroline had to go through the story still again.

"Caroline, that was dumb!" said Eddie. "The boys probably haven't had such a good laugh in years! Why didn't you wait till Beth and I could come too?"

"I just wanted so much to see what was down there."

"Josh and Jake are probably—" Eddie stopped suddenly. "Listen, I've got an idea! I'm going to call the Hatfords and ask to talk to their parents. I'm going to say that you're missing, and we wondered if Wally has seen you since school let out."

"Oh, *do* it, Eddie!" Caroline began to feel better. That would really shake the boys up a little. Maybe it had been worth climbing down that trapdoor after all. "See you soon," she said, "but come and get me if I don't show up."

She headed for the back of the store. Beth was right. There must be a back door someplace. She put her hands out in front of her and made her way along the aisle. Past the picture-book tent, and on into the stockroom that was black as coal. There was only a small square of half-light at the very back, and at last Caroline reached the door to the alley.

There was a long push-down bar on the door, and Caroline pushed. The door opened, but immediately the air was filled with a head-splitting sound. *Burglar alarm!*

Almost as soon as the door opened it began closing again, and Caroline barely escaped out into the alley. The door went shut on the hem of her jacket, and Caroline felt a soft tug as she jerked her jacket free and ran as fast as she could down the alley toward home.

On and on the alarm went, clanging like a four-alarm fire. An alarm she could hear all the way down the street.

Her sides hurt from running, but Caroline did not stop until she was on the road bridge leading to Island Avenue. Then she looked around. A police car was racing down Main Street, siren wailing. It began to slow as it neared Oldakers' Bookstore, and finally came to a stop.

Caroline turned and ran on home. She walked in just as Mother was saying, "Where's Caroline?" and then her father's voice, "Well, *some*thing's going on downtown. Listen to that siren! Better not be any of the fellas on my team getting hurt before the big game."

"Dinner ready?" Caroline said casually, leaving the screwdriver and flashlight in the closet along with her jacket, and walking into the dining room. She exchanged quick smiles with Beth and Eddie.

"Yes. Wash your hands and get the salad," said Mother.

Fifteen

▽

Abaguchie?

Wally felt sick. He left the dinner table and went upstairs to his room, lying across his bed on his stomach, listening to the wail of the siren in the distance.

GIRL FOUND DEAD IN CELLAR OF BOOKSTORE. He could see the headlines even now. GIRL TRAPPED IN CELLAR SUFFO-CATES. The possibilities were unlimited. BOY CHARGED WITH MURDER. BOYS' PRANKS COST GIRL'S LIFE. HATFORD BOY GETS LIFE SENTENCE. Wally moaned.

The noise of the police siren stopped. Now they were discovering the body. Now they were loading it into an ambulance. Now they were unclenching the fingers of the dead girl, and there was a folded piece of paper with only three words: *Wally did it.*

Jake and Josh came upstairs next and sat down silently on the edge of Wally's bed.

"You know what happened, I'll bet?" said Jake.

"Somebody saw her trying to get out of Oldakers' and thought she was trying to rob it and shot her."

"Shut up!" said Wally. "Just shut up."

Peter appeared in the doorway. "Maybe the abaguchie got her," he said, his face sober.

"Listen, that siren might not have anything to do with Caroline at all. She probably crawled out and left as soon as we went home," said Josh.

"Then why did Eddie call here and wonder if I'd seen her?" Wally asked.

"Oh. Right," said Josh.

"Maybe the abaguchie ate her up," said Peter.

"Shut up!" Wally said again. "If you guys can't say anything helpful, don't say anything at all."

Mother's voice sounded below in the hallway: "Are you boys all through eating? I swear, isn't anyone hungry tonight?"

"I'm all done, Mom," Wally called.

"Me too," said Josh and Jake together.

"*I'm* having *dessert!*" Peter announced, and went on back downstairs.

"We could be in big, big trouble," said Wally.

"Maybe we ought to walk over to the police station and turn ourselves in," said Josh.

The boys looked at each other. Somehow it seemed the only sensible thing to do. Just explain exactly what had happened before the sheriff came looking.

They went downstairs. "We're going to walk into town and see what's happening, Mom," said Jake.

"Now, don't you boys get to fooling around and waste the whole evening," she said. "I want your homework done before nine o'clock."

"Be right back," Jake told her.

Wally said nothing. He was thinking how their last words to her would be "Be right back," and twenty years later they'd get out of prison.

They put on their jackets and went outside, where the wind was even colder than they had remembered. As they walked toward the business district, they could see the light on the police cruiser going around and around.

Wally kept listening for the sound of an ambulance. The sound of an ambulance would mean that Caroline was still alive and they were rushing her to a hospital. No ambulance meant that she was dead when they found her, and they were just waiting for the coroner to get there. *Why* did the Malloys have to move to Buckman anyway? Life was so easy and simple before they came!

He had to get this over with. Had to know if she was dead or alive. He found himself half running as they reached Main Street, and ran up the sidewalk to Oldakers' where a small crowd had gathered. People seemed to be going in and out, so the boys went inside and through the store to the back. There stood their father beside the police chief, a reporter, the older Mr. Oldaker, and several others.

"What happened?" Wally skidded to a stop beside his dad.

"Can't quite say," the police chief told him. "Burglar alarm went off here at Oldakers', but there doesn't seem to be anything missing."

Wally went limp with relief. "Nobody hurt?" he asked.

The police chief looked at him curiously. "No," he said. "Why would there be?"

"I think the burglar was frightened off by the alarm," said Mr. Oldaker. "I figured nobody would break in the front door, because they'd have to break the glass. So I put the burglar alarm on the back, and when it goes off, you know it."

"And you're sure nothing is missing?" the police chief asked.

"Not unless it was a book or two. We empty the cash register every night. Typewriter's still there. The adding machine . . . What else would a burglar want?"

The reporter, however, was bending over the back door. He was scraping his ballpoint pen along the edge of the doorway.

"Look here," he said to the police chief.

"What have you got?"

Mr. Hatford and the police chief stooped down to

see. Wally edged closer to his father. The reporter was holding a tuft of light brown fur between his thumb and forefinger.

When the newspaper came out the next day, there was a story on page one:

> An apparent burglary was attempted and failed last night at Oldakers' Bookstore on Main when the alarm went off as the back door was opened. No items were reported missing, but there was no explanation for a tuft of brown fur that seemed to have been caught as the door was closing. . . .

Mr. Hatford grinned a little when he read the story aloud at breakfast.

"The abaguchie has stopped carrying off cats now, and is devouring books, perhaps?" he said.

∇ • ∇ • ∇ • ∇ • ∇ • ∇ • ∇ • ∇ • ∇ • ∇ • ∇

Sixteen

∇

Playing Ball

Things turned out even better than Caroline had dreamed. Mr. Oldaker had not caught her coming up out of his cellar because he'd already gone home; the boys had not succeeded in trapping her there for long; and somehow, in making her escape, she had accidentally started a whole new rumor about the abaguchie; the only thing it had cost her was a little tuft of fur from the hem of Beth's old jacket. Was life in Buckman wonderful or what?

Eddie's thumb had recovered enough by the weekend that she wanted to practice her batting and pitching again, so once more the three girls made their way to the field behind the college. This time, however, they were not alone. The Hatford boys had got there first. Jake was pitching, Wally was catcher, Josh was up at bat, and Peter's job seemed to be to go after the ball wherever it went.

"What do *you* want?" Jake yelled when he saw the girls. "Scram!"

"We have as much right to be here as you do," Beth said. "You don't own this field."

Just then Jake pitched, Josh swung his bat, and the ball came whizzing right over to where the girls were standing. Eddie simply put out one hand and caught it in her glove, as easily as if she were answering the phone.

Caroline could see by the look on the boys' faces that they were getting ready for an argument over the ball, when Eddie threw it back to Jake.

Whoosh! Jake caught it, but barely. He blinked.

Without a word he threw it to Josh again. This time Josh hit it hard and it went sailing out into center field. Peter ran and ran, and Josh could have gone around the diamond three times before the ball got back to Jake again.

"So what do you want?" asked Wally, still staring at the girls.

"I came over to practice," said Eddie. "You want us to be your basemen?"

"We don't need any girls," Wally told them.

But they clearly needed basemen. Jake and Josh looked at each other. Then Jake gave a sly grin, as though it were all a joke.

"Sure! Let 'em be our basemen! Why not?" he said, tongue in cheek.

Eddie walked over to first and said she'd cover right field. Caroline took second and center field, and Beth took third and covered left field. Peter moved up to shortstop.

Josh took another turn at bat and made a home run while Caroline was running after the ball.

Jake and Josh exchanged places, and Jake made it to second while Peter fumbled the ball.

Wally took his place at bat, while Josh pitched, and made it to first.

Without any teams or any lineup the boys kept batting and running, until finally Peter sat down on the ground and said he was tired of the game.

"Well, see you later," Jake said to the girls as he gathered up his bat and ball.

"What do you mean?" said Eddie. "Aren't you going to field for us? Don't *we* get some batting practice?"

"Time for dinner," Josh said, and the boys all laughed.

"Why, those rotten rats!" said Beth. "We ran our legs off out here and they're not even going to give you a chance, Eddie!"

Eddie glared after them. "I'm going to make that team, don't think I won't," she said.

·

There was a football game that weekend, Buckman versus Salem. Caroline and her sisters and their mother went as usual, and sat in some of the best seats on the fifty-yard line. Caroline knew all the Buckman College cheers by heart, so that if she *didn't* succeed as an actress when she was grown, she might be a professional cheerleader instead. The problem was that she got so caught up in the cheers that she shouted them louder than anyone else, and sometimes even sprang to her feet, fists in the air, when the cheerleaders did their final handsprings at the end.

> Two bits, four bits,
> Six bits, a dollar;
> All for Buckman
> Stand up and holler.
> Yeaaah, *team*!

Or:

> What do we want?
> *Touchdown!*
> When do we want it?
> *Now!*

To which Caroline leapt to her feet, and added:

> What do we do to Salem?
> *Biff! Bam! Pow!*

"Caroline, for goodness' sake, sit down," said Mother, yanking her arm. "Must you act like a pagan?"

A pagan? Caroline instantly fell in love with the word. A pagan to her meant a wild, mysterious woman with a primitive soul, sort of a female abaguchie. Or maybe a princess. A pagan princess, worshiping the sun, who had to escape because she was going to be sacrificed to the deity to make crops grow or something.

She got so wrapped up in her fantasy that when she saw a player intercept the ball and make a touchdown, she cheered before she realized it was the opposing team.

"That does it, I'm going for a Coke," said Eddie. "I'm too embarrassed to sit on the same bench with her." She made her way past a row of knees, little white clouds of breath coming out of people's mouths, Beth behind her, and Caroline bringing up the rear.

"Not you, Caroline!" Eddie said, when she saw her sister following along.

"I won't cheer, I promise," Caroline said.

They went down to the concession stand and bought Cokes, and as they were standing in the milling crowd, sloshing the ice around in the tall paper cups, Beth gave Caroline a nudge.

"Look."

Caroline turned and, on down the fence, saw Jake and Wally hanging over the top, watching the game. And then, as the girls stared, Jake's and Wally's heads disappeared, and Peter's and Josh's appeared in their place.

"You know what they're doing?" Beth cried delightedly. "They're taking turns standing on each other's shoulders and watching from over the fence."

"Definitely illegal," said Eddie.

Caroline sloshed the ice some more. "So what if we sneaked up behind them and dumped our ice down the necks of the guys on the bottom?"

"Perfect!" giggled Beth.

They went out the gate and made their way around to where the boys were standing, just as Beth said, on each other's shoulders. Peter and Josh were on top, Wally and Jake on the bottom.

"Ready, set, go!" Eddie whispered, and the girls crept up behind them and dropped the ice from their cups down the collars of Wally and Jake.

It was all over in a minute. Wally and Jake reared back, Peter and Josh tumbled on top of them, and the girls ran pell mell back to the gate, but were stopped by the security guard.

"We were just in there!" Caroline explained. "We only came out for a minute."

"Ticket stubs?" said the guard.

Caroline looked at her sisters. Mother had them!

"We—we left them with Mom," said Beth.

"Sorry," said the guard. "Can't let you in without the stubs."

"But we're—" Eddie stopped. The girls all knew that their father did not like them trying to get special privileges by using his name, but this was an emergency. "We're Coach Malloy's daughters."

"Coach Malloy's daughters, and they don't even know enough to keep their ticket stubs? Coach Malloy's daughters, and they'd leave right in the middle of the game? I doubt it," said the guard.

In the background the Hatford boys hooted derisively.

What happened was that the girls had to hang around the gate until the game was over, because the Hatford boys were lying in wait for them if they had tried to walk home. Caroline hoped that Mother would come looking for them, but she didn't, and they were tired and cold and cranky when the game ended at last, a three-point win by Buckman, and Mother came out with the crowd.

"Where on earth did you go? Did you see the field goal in the last two minutes of the game?"

"We went out the gate and the guard wouldn't let us back in," said Beth. "All we want is to go home."

Mother got out the car keys.

"Well, for heaven's sake, then, you should have

gone on home. Why were you hanging around?" she asked. And then, without waiting for an answer, she said, "You know, I am really beginning to like this little town. I met a number of faculty members tonight, and it's so nice being called by my first name."

The girls piled into the car. "In fact," said Mother, "I'm feeling very comfortable with the community in general. Do you know where we're going for Thanksgiving this year?"

"Ohio?" Caroline guessed.

"No, I got a call from Mrs. Hatford this morning. We're invited over there."

Caroline stared at her sisters. *The* Hatfords? The Horrible Hatfords? *Them?*

"I think it's wonderful. She said she knew we didn't have any relatives down here, and if we weren't going back to Ohio for Thanksgiving we were welcome at their table. I told her we'd love to come, and I'd bring the pies."

There was no sound at all from the backseat. To have to sit behind Wally Hatford every day for the rest of fourth grade was bad enough, Caroline thought, but to have to sit across the table from him at Thanksgiving and be nice?

"Do we have a choice?" Eddie asked after a minute.

"No, you do not," Mother said.

Seventeen

▽

Letters

If it was distressing to Caroline, Beth, and Eddie, to the Hatford boys it was a shock. They positively bellowed when Mother told them the news.

"What?" Wally's eyes almost popped out of his head.

"Wally, stop shouting!" said his mother. "Aunt Ida and Uncle Bob are going to North Carolina for Thanksgiving this year, and it just wouldn't seem right not to have a crowd around the table. Mrs. Malloy was so pleased when I called and invited them to come."

As if that weren't enough, a letter arrived from the Benson boys down in Georgia:

Dear Wally (and Jake, Josh, and Peter):
You guys getting all ready for Thanksgiving? Boy,
we are having a feast. Mom made reservations at this

99

sort of southern mansion where it takes almost three hours to eat a meal, and there are supposed to be thirty different desserts to choose from and you eat as much as you want. I'll make a list of everything we eat and send it to you, and tell you whether I barfed later or not.

It's not cold here like it gets in Buckman. Yesterday I went to school without a jacket. Danny has this real good-looking teacher who rides a bike to school some days. She had a flat tire and Danny fixed it for her, and she gave him some chocolates. I mean, can you imagine old Applebaum giving anyone chocolates?

There are seventeen boys in my class and only eight girls. This is probably the very best year I ever had in school. Fun, I mean.

How are you guys doing, anyway? What are you going to do for Thanksgiving? Write sometime.

        Bill (and Danny, Steve, Tony, and Doug)

Dear Bill (and Danny, Steve, Tony, and Doug):

You want to know what we're doing for Thanksgiving? Just because you guys left Buckman for Georgia and rented your house to a Whomper, a Weirdo, and a Crazie, we've got to eat Thanksgiving dinner with them. Mom invited those girls over here! I can't believe this. It is going to be the worst Thanksgiving I ever had in my life, and if you guys don't come back soon, I don't know what we'll do.

I think you're just nuts about that teacher. I think just because she gave Danny chocolates when he fixed her bike, she's making you all sort of nuts. Have you forgotten all the fun we had here? Have you forgotten all the things we've done together in Buckman? Especially, have you read anything in the newspapers there about the abaguchie? Bet you haven't. There's even a new rumor that it got in the bookstore somehow.

If you want to know more about the abaguchie you have to come back. You have to hear it with your own ears.

COME HOME NOW!!!!

> *Wally (and Jake, Josh, and Peter)*

P.S. We mean it, guys!

Eighteen

▽

Paw Prints

It was Eddie's idea, actually. It had rained Saturday morning—a cold November rain—gray sky over gray trees over a gray landscape—the kind of day that made Eddie wish for baseball summers, Beth to wish for warm July days of hammock reading, and Caroline to fantasize herself under bright lights in a packed auditorium, with her name, of course, on the marquee.

"What we need," Eddie said, lying on the floor, tossing a baseball up in the air and catching it while flat on her back, "is something that would make a great paw print. We could go over to the Hatfords' after dark and make paw prints in the wet ground, right up that dirt path to their back door."

It was a better idea than Caroline had ever thought of herself, and Beth—who lived half her life inside her head along with vampires and headless horsemen—at once put her mind to the kind of paw prints an abaguchie might make.

They went outside to experiment in the damp earth of Mother's empty flower bed, and discovered that by pressing the palm of their hands down in the dirt, then using the thumb to make prints for the toes, they had a good imitation of an animal's paw print—something resembling the print of a large cat.

After that they worked to make it look real, placing the paw prints almost in front of each other, the way a large cat might go slinking about.

Evening could not come quickly enough. There had been a lot more talk of the abaguchie since the small tuft of Caroline's fur trim had been found along the door frame at Oldakers'. Not a day went by at school that someone didn't mention it, and Caroline and her sisters could not think of a better way to keep the story alive than to place some odd paw prints where the Hatford boys would find them.

Why the Hatfords? Who else was as much fun to tease, trick, fool, annoy, harass, and just plain drive to distraction? And things could not have gone more perfectly when Mother announced that there was chili on the stove for dinner, bagels for toasting with cheese, a salad in the fridge, and everyone could eat when ready. She was working on new curtains for the sun-room, and did not want to stop and put a formal meal on the table.

The girls ate early and then, when it was almost, but not quite, dark, set out in dark jeans, socks, sweaters, and gloves. When they got across the bridge, the Hatford house was ablaze with lights. Every room, thought Caroline, was like a stage, and you could walk around the entire house and decide what stage you wanted to watch.

"The main thing," Eddie whispered, "is to be sure all the Hatfords are inside. We don't want any surprises—no one walking up behind us."

Everybody was inside. Jake was watching TV. Mrs. Hatford and Wally were making dinner, and Josh was standing in the kitchen doorway. Mr. Hatford was reading to Peter on the couch.

In case any of the Hatfords were coming out later, the girls decided to start at the steps and work backward—across the lawn, through the empty flower bed, over to the bare earth around the driveway, and out the gate behind the shed. Wherever they could plant a paw print, they would. Beth and Eddie made the prints, and Caroline led the way, keeping an eye on the house.

It would have been better, of course, if they'd had a flashlight to admire their work as they went along, but they had practiced enough in Mother's flower bed at home to know in what direction the toes should be pointing, and about how far apart the prints should be.

"Wait!" Caroline cautioned at one point when Mr. Hatford came to the window and looked out over the darkened landscape, hands in his pockets. The girls crouched, ready to run if the door opened, but after a while he ambled off again, and when Caroline next checked, he was eating dinner.

They completed the garden plot and started in on the bare spots along the driveway.

"We shouldn't make a steady line of prints," Beth said. "A big cat would probably step off into the grass now and then."

Silently the girls worked on, moving in the direction where Caroline was standing. If only it didn't rain again before morning, destroying their handiwork. *One* of the Hatfords should notice those prints on Sunday when they all came out for church.

They had finished the bare dirt along the driveway and were moving off toward the trees when Caroline heard a twig snap somewhere behind the toolshed.

She wheeled quickly around and listened. Nothing.

"Did you hear something?" whispered Beth.

"Wait. . . ." said Eddie.

The girls froze, not daring to make a sound.

This time there was a crackle of underbrush, like a swift movement back in the weeds near the trees. Caroline turned some more and saw two yellow eyes about three feet from the ground, staring right at her.

The scream came in spite of herself.

"Caroline!" said Eddie just as Beth rose up from a crouch. A low growl came from the direction of the eyes.

And suddenly Caroline was running pell-mell toward the house. Unmindful of the consequences, she tumbled onto the steps. She realized too late that Beth and Eddie were still out on the driveway.

"Caroline!" she heard Eddie whisper just as the porch light came on and Mr. Hatford stepped out, followed by Wally, then Jake and Josh.

"What's happening?" asked the boys' father.

"There's . . . something out there!" gasped Caroline. "We saw two eyes! Two yellow eyes about this far off the ground!" She put out one hand.

Beth came over. "It growled," she added.

"Out where?" asked Mr. Hatford, coming down the steps.

Mrs. Hatford appeared with a flashlight, followed by Peter. The boys stared at the girls.

"What were you doing out here?" asked Wally.

Now Eddie came over. "We were just cutting through your yard—"

"Look here!" yelled Wally, taking the flashlight and coming down the steps. "Hey, Dad, look at these prints!"

"M'gosh!" cried Jake. "They're huge!"

The boys stared at the girls some more. And then Wally must have noticed their muddy hands, and the mud on Beth's and Eddie's knees, because he yelled, "It's all a trick! They've been over here making paw prints in the dirt, and they screamed to make us think something's out there."

"Something was!" cried Caroline, not even caring now. "Yes, we *did* make the paw prints, just as a joke, but when we got back in the weeds, we *did* see something. We *did* hear a growl!"

"Sure, and it snows in July," said Wally.

"It's true!" said Beth.

Mr. Hatford smiled a little. "Well, girls, do you want the boys to walk you home?"

"No," said Eddie. "We were just leaving."

"Hey, nice paw prints!" Jake chortled.

"Good try," said Josh.

Caroline and her sisters headed for the swinging bridge.

"I was never so humiliated in my life!" said Eddie. "Caroline, why did you scream? After all our work, you ruined it."

"But I saw eyes, Eddie! You saw them, too, Beth. You know you did."

"And I heard the growl," Beth insisted.

"We'll never live this down," Eddie told them. "Our big chance, and we blew it."

Nineteen

∇

Two Yellow Eyes

The boys hooted as the girls headed down the driveway toward the road and the swinging bridge on the other side.

"They actually thought we'd fall for that!" said Wally. "They must think we're really dumb."

The four boys followed the paw prints around the yard, laughing at all the work the girls had done to make them think the abaguchie had been there.

"The thing is," Wally said when they went back inside again, "Beth was really scared. Caroline too. I don't think they were faking it."

"Even Eddie looked worried," Jake agreed. "Maybe they *did* see something."

"Could have been a dog or a fox or a deer or something. Two yellow eyes could be almost anything," Josh told them.

After dinner, however, while Jake and Josh were

playing a video game, and Peter was taking his bath,
Wally put on his jacket and went out in the backyard
with the flashlight. For a long time he stood at the
bottom of the steps and just watched and listened. If
there was any creature back in the trees behind the
shed, he decided, and if he waited long enough, he
would hear something. See something. No animal
could be one hundred percent quiet, could it? When
he heard something, he'd turn on the flashlight, see
what it was.

Caroline was a good actress, but she wasn't *that*
good. Wally thought he knew fear when he saw it. It
was possible that the girls had made the prints and
then put on a show of acting scared to make the
Hatfords think something was really back there, but
no: they would have brushed off their hands and
knees.

Standing absolutely still out in the November cold
made his legs seem to lock into position, like those
of a horse asleep on its feet. Wally wondered what it
was like to be a sentry or guard on duty who would
be shot if he went to sleep at his post. He had been
standing there only ten minutes, perhaps. What if he
were on watch for ten hours? What if the safety of
the whole camp depended on whether he saw the
faintest light, heard the slightest sound . . .

His knees felt frozen. He needed to move, and he
began to get a little braver. He had been out this

long and heard nothing. Why didn't he go back as far as the trees behind the toolshed, where Caroline said they had seen the eyes, and just stand quietly *there* for fifteen minutes? Then if he still saw or heard nothing, he would figure the girls hadn't seen anything either.

Softly, he moved across the damp grass and stood leaning against the back of the toolshed, hands in his pockets, shoulders hunched against the chill. There were goose bumps all up and down his legs where the wind whipped his trousers against him.

For a moment he thought he heard something, a whine, perhaps. Then he realized it was the whistle of the wind.

How long had he been standing here now? Five minutes? Ten? He began counting to sixty to keep track of the minutes, but after a while forgot which minute he was counting off—seven or eight. After that he felt he was too numb to think; even his brain was freezing.

Something snapped back in the trees, like a twig breaking underfoot.

Wally stiffened, his eyes searching out the darkness. A small forest creature scurrying home?

Snap. Again the sound, like a footstep. Then a rustle, as though something was rooting about, pawing the ground. Sniffing.

Wally knew if he ran for the house to get Jake and

Josh he would frighten away the visitor. If he did not run for the house, he might have a heart attack on the spot. Wally did not run, not because he was brave but because he felt his feet and legs were icicles.

The air was quiet. Wally heard only the thump of his heart, the thrubbing of blood in his temples. And then, not ten yards away, two yellow eyes stared out at Wally from the trees—two yellow eyes, close together, about three feet from the ground. They moved to the left as though the creature were circling, but then they stopped and moved to the right.

Wally inched backward toward the door of the shed, heart racing, mouth dry, fingers clutching the flashlight.

Turn on the flashlight! his brain told him, *and see what it is. Now's your chance! Turn on the light!*

No, run! his feet argued. *Forget the light and run, stupid!*

He would get to the door of the shed and *then* turn on the light, he decided. If necessary he could jump inside and close the door after him.

The yellow eyes seemed to come closer still.

In terror Wally reached the corner of the shed and lifted the flashlight, but his hands were so cold, he dropped it. And in that split second the yellow eyes disappeared.

Frantically, Wally picked up the light and shone it

in the direction of the eyes, but there was nothing. He took a few steps forward, disappointment overcoming fear, and even rattled the branches of a nearby bush, hoping to flush the creature out if it was still lurking about, but he didn't see anything at all.

The grove of trees behind the shed seemed empty now. As sure as Wally had felt before that a presence was there, a creature unseen, he now knew that it was gone. He turned and kicked the shed hard, only injuring his toe, and limped back to the house, wiping his nose with one hand. *Stupid, stupid, stupid!*

Coming into the kitchen, he found his brothers making popcorn in the microwave.

"Where have *you* been?" asked Josh.

Wally slumped down on a chair, still shaking in his jacket. "I saw them," he said, lips barely moving.

"The girls are back?" asked Jake.

Wally shook his head. "The eyes. The yellow eyes."

"What?"

"But when I turned on the flashlight, they were gone."

"Maybe you only imagined it," Josh said.

"No! I saw two yellow eyes. They were three feet off the ground, just like Caroline said. And I heard something moving around, sort of sniffing and snorting in the underbrush. I *know* something was out there. The girls *did* see it, only I don't know what it was."

Jake and Josh sat down slowly in the chairs around the table, and only Peter remembered the popcorn and got it out of the microwave in time.

"If it's there," Josh said after a minute, "we're going to catch it."

Twenty

▽

A Little Talk
with Wally

It was miserable having Eddie mad at her. It wasn't so bad when Beth was angry, because all you had to do to make up to Beth was hand her a new book, and within minutes she was lost in another time and place and had forgotten what the argument was about.

Eddie, however, did not like being made to look like a fool. She did not appreciate appearing foolish in front of girlfriends, but especially did not like to look stupid in front of boys, the Hatford boys in particular. And when Eddie was upset, she simply stayed after school to shoot baskets in the all-purpose room, or came home to bounce a ball off the side of the garage, and whatever Caroline suggested, she'd say simply "That's dumb."

If Caroline was again to have the support of her oldest sister, she was going to have to do something rather dramatic, she decided. Something that *worked*. Something braver than even Eddie would have thought of to do, but Caroline hadn't a clue as to what that might be.

At school on Monday, however, she got a break because, for the first time since she had moved to Buckman, Wally Hatford turned around in his chair, all on his own, and talked to her. Politely.

"What exactly did you see at the back of our yard the other night?" he asked.

Caroline didn't answer right away because she wasn't sure what he was going to do with her answer.

"We were only kidding around," she said. "It was just something to do."

"I know, but you really did see something, didn't you?"

"I'm not sure," Caroline told him. Were they having a real conversation? Was it possible that a Hatford boy and a Malloy girl could actually behave like normal people when they wanted to?

"Did you hear anything, then?"

"Yes. Twigs snapping, I think. Like someone—some*thing*—was walking on them. And maybe a . . . well, sort of snuffing sound."

"That's what *I* heard!" Wally said.

"When?"

Now Wally looked uncomfortable, as though he couldn't trust *her* with the answer. But he must have decided to take a chance, because he said at last, "After you went home that night, I stood out by the back of the shed and watched."

Caroline felt her eyes growing larger. "What did you see?"

"I'm not sure either," said Wally. "Did you really see two yellow eyes?"

"Well . . ." Caroline thought hard. "I saw *some-*thing. It certainly looked like two yellow eyes, and I heard something."

"Me too," said Wally. "What did it sound like?"

"Well . . ." And again Caroline thought. How much was real and how much might she have only imagined? "I heard growling. Maybe just one growl. It could have been the wind, I guess."

"But you don't think so?"

"I don't know what to think," Caroline told him, as honest as she'd ever been in her life. "But Beth said she heard growling too."

"Well, *I* think you really did see and hear some-thing. I did too. And if something *was* back there, Jake and Josh and I are going to capture it."

Now Caroline's eyes were *really* wide. Was this a trick? She didn't think so. Still, with all the things the Hatford boys had pulled in the past . . .

"How?" she asked.

"We're going to build a cage and put bait in it," Wally said. "Josh made a drawing, and we're going to build it tonight. If we catch anything, I'll let you know."

She couldn't believe her ears. "Thanks," she said.

After school that day Caroline was disturbed that Eddie still would rather play basketball in the all-purpose room than walk home with her and Beth. Caroline hated the thought that Eddie might think she was getting too old for them—might go off and spend all her time with someone else.

She glanced over at Beth, but Beth, as usual, had her nose stuck in a book. What would happen to the Malloy sisters if Eddie didn't hang around with her and Beth anymore? All Caroline's plans for a movie-production company called Malloy Enterprises would just float right out the window.

If only she could do something splendid and brave, like capturing the abaguchie barehanded, to make Eddie proud of her again. *Proud* to say that Caroline was her sister. If she couldn't do that, she would settle for *sighting* the abaguchie. But even that was farfetched.

Then she had another idea. What about making the Hatford boys believe the abaguchie had come to their trap and taken their bait? And after the boys spread the story around school, she'd tell them what really happened. Maybe even keep the bait as evidence.

As soon as Caroline thought of it, however, she felt guilty. Wally had let her in on a secret, and look what she was about to do. On the other hand, when had Wally ever let her in on a secret before when it wasn't a trick of some sort?

This would pay him back for pulling the chair out from under her in the Halloween play, for trying to throw her in the river at Smuggler's Cove, for dropping dead birds and fish on the Malloy side of the river, locking her in the toolshed, trapping her in Oldakers' cellar . . .

The longer the list grew, the more Caroline began to feel that this little trick was nothing at all compared to all Wally Hatford had done to her—Wally and his brothers. And as soon as she made up her mind that she was going to make them think an abaguchie had come and gone, she knew exactly how she was going to do it.

Twenty-one

▽

Bait

Wally decided he had better not tell his brothers about his talk with Caroline. He didn't know why he had told her so much himself. Because he really wanted to know if she had seen anything, he guessed. Anyway, what harm would it do? She and her sisters—she and Beth, anyway—had really been scared. If Wally could capture an abaguchie and find out what it *really* was, maybe the Malloy girls would quit bugging them—would realize that they weren't to be messed with and would leave them alone. And if the Benson brothers heard about it down in Georgia, you bet your boots they'd come back!

By the time Wally got home from school, because it was his day to clean all the erasers for Miss Applebaum, he found Jake and Josh at the kitchen table with Josh's elaborate drawing of the abaguchie trap. Peter was leaning his elbows on the end of the table, a piece of bread smeared with peanut butter in his hands, chewing wide eyed with his mouth open.

Wally tried not to look. Whenever Wally was really hungry at school and didn't think he could hold out until noon, he thought about the way half-chewed bread and peanut butter looked in Peter's mouth, and he wasn't hungry anymore.

From where Wally sat across the table, he could see a drawing of a big rectangular box being held up with a stick.

"Where do we get the box?"

"Mom said there was a wooden refrigerator crate at the hardware store she could save for us."

Josh turned the paper around so Wally could see better.

"We put the bait under here, see, so the animal has to crawl under to get it. But we'll have a trip wire attached to the bait, so all the abaguchie has to do is jiggle it a little and the crate will come down on top of him."

"We won't even know what we've got!" Jake said. "We'll all be too scared to lift it up, and if we did, the animal could get out."

Josh thought about that. "Then we'll have to drill little holes in the sides so we can see in. Maybe even a bigger hole so we can feed it till the sheriff comes or something."

"How are we supposed to get that refrigerator crate home, Josh?" Wally asked. "They're heavy!"

"Carry it. All four of us. When you're ready, we'll go."

Wally liked any excuse at all to go to the hardware store, because it was like three stores in one—three storefront shops, all connected to each other by doorways on the inside—one selling refrigerators and other appliances, one selling lamps and dishes, and the third selling nails and seeds and paint. Wally liked the one selling nails and seeds and paint. He liked to watch the clerks measure out seeds on the old metal scales—first putting the right weight on one side, then adding the seeds to the scoop on the other until the two sides balanced.

There were times Wally thought he might like to spend his life just working the scales, measuring things until everything balanced out right, because so often nothing in his life seemed to balance at all.

"You fellas want that wooden refrigerator crate, huh?" the owner said. "Gonna have a tree house or something?"

"Something like that," Jake said.

Mother, who was working the cash register, told them where to find it, and five minutes later the four boys were carrying it home on their shoulders like a coffin.

It took a long time to set it up. They worked right

up until dinnertime, and when Mother came home from the hardware store, she said she'd delay supper another half hour so that they could finish, seeing how much work they had put in on the project. She was as interested as anyone else in what they might catch. Put that abaguchie rumor to rest once and for all.

At last, with Wally holding the flashlight and Peter jumping up and down because he was cold, they rigged the large heavy crate so that one end rested on the ground back by the trees, the other held up by a stick. On the underside a raw chicken leg dangled from a wire. If anything pulled at the chicken leg, the wire would pull the stick out from under the uplifted end of the crate, and the creature would be trapped. At the same time a cowbell attached to the crate would clang, so the boys would know something was there.

They were so excited, they could scarcely eat dinner. They had tried it out again and again, each taking turns being the abaguchie, and each time the crate came down over them.

But Wally suddenly sat straight up in his chair. "It could be *any*thing!" he said in dismay. "A rat could get under that crate and nibble that chicken leg and the crate would fall. We could have done all that work for a rat."

"I don't know," said Josh. "The meat's hanging,

remember, and it's about three feet off the ground. It's got to be a creature big enough to get at the meat and give it a good tug."

Wally passed the potatoes. Jake passed the meat. And just at that moment, from far out in the backyard, came the clang of the cowbell.

Twenty-two

▽

The Capture

Caroline sat on her bed with her jacket—Beth's outgrown jacket—on her legs and wondered where she would do the least damage.

There was already a small bare spot along the hem where a tuft of the brownish fur had caught in the back door of Oldakers' Bookstore. She could not afford to lose another piece of fur there.

The cuffs of the sleeves? Or fur from the edge of the pocket?

Turning the jacket inside out, she found a place inside the collar where it didn't seem to make any difference, and then she reached for the scissors.

Wrong! That could make it look too even. The fur had to be torn away, as though snagged from the coat of a mountain lion. Carefully she tugged and twisted out a piece of fur, a larger piece than she'd intended, but it certainly looked real.

She had been coming out of the library when she'd seen Wally and his brothers carrying a huge refrigerator crate down the alley from the hardware store. She had waited behind a wall until they passed. *That* must be the cage Wally had been talking about. Not only was that the cage but it was big and strong enough to ship the abaguchie off to a zoo in, once they'd caught it!

She spent the rest of the afternoon at home, knowing she could not go see what they had done until she was sure they were having dinner. Finally, she stuck the tuft of fur inside her pocket and set off. No flashlight. She couldn't afford having them catch her this time. She crossed the swinging bridge and slipped around the back of the Hatfords' house.

Her heart began to pound harder as she faced the dark line of trees behind the toolshed where she had seen—or thought she had seen—two yellow eyes, and heard—or thought she'd heard—a growl. Did she dare go back there again without a flashlight? She wished now she had brought one. But she *had* to go. She had to do something incredibly brave so that Eddie would think it fun to hang around with her again.

She groped her way toward the shed, almost entangling herself in Mrs. Hatford's clothesline, and stumbling once over Peter's wagon, but she managed to get back to the shed without anyone hearing, and looked around.

It didn't take long to make out the large refrigerator crate back in the trees, one end propped up with a stick.

She could tell right away what was supposed to happen. The abaguchie would crawl under the box, eat the bait, and somehow knock over the stick so that the crate would drop and trap it. What she had to do was crawl underneath, unhook the bait, and leave the piece of fake fur in its place, being careful to get in and out without knocking over the stick that was holding up one end of the crate.

Was this going to be easy or what?

Caroline got down on her hands and knees and crawled under the heavy wood crate, careful not to touch the stick at the other end. She was beginning to think—no, she had thought for a long time, actually—that girls were far smarter than boys. Obviously the Hatfords thought that if they went to all this work to rig up the trap, the abaguchie would come right along and crawl in. If the abaguchie was clever enough to keep from being captured so far, wouldn't it be clever enough not to get captured now? And there were dozens of other animals that could crawl in here and eat the bait, so that all this trap might catch would be a squirrel or something.

No, girls were superior to boys in every way. If

you took all of Jake's and Josh's and Wally's and Peter's talents and put them together, they still wouldn't measure up to half of Eddie's skill in sports, Beth's mind, or Caroline's imagination.

Her fingers felt around for the bait, and for a moment she felt as though this might be too much for her. What if it was a dead bird or fish? A live mouse?

Something bumped against her cheek. Gingerly she reached up and felt something cold and slippery and raw-smelling hanging from a wire. Ugh! But it didn't move, so at least it wasn't alive.

Her fingers explored it. A chicken leg, they told her. A raw chicken leg. That wasn't so bad. All she had to do was pull it off, stick the clump of fake fur in its place, and crawl out again.

She yanked on the leg.

Clang, clang, clang!

Caroline did not know what was happening or how, but from somewhere just beyond her head a loud bell was sounding, then the crate came down around her.

Frantically she tried to lift up one side of the crate, but somehow the chicken-leg wire had got tangled in her hair. She was trying to free herself when she heard yells, running footsteps, and then cautious voices outside the box.

"We did it!" A yell from Wally.

"Josh, it worked!" Jake's voice. "Listen, we've got to be careful, now."

"Who's got the flashlight?"

"Peter, go get the flashlight."

"Why do I have to do everything?"

"Do you hear anything?"

"Maybe we should get Dad."

"We can at least peek."

More footsteps. These seemed to be going back to the house. The slam of a door. Then another slam, and footsteps were coming back again.

"Give it to me."

"Turn it on."

"Careful, now."

And suddenly a beam of light came through a round hole on the far side of the box, and then there was a gasp, and a chorus of voices:

"Caroline!"

Twenty-three

▽

Gone

Wally didn't know if he was more pleased or disappointed. A couple of months ago he would have wanted nothing more than to trap Crazy Caroline under a box and keep her there an hour or so, just to get even for all the stuff the Malloy sisters had pulled on him.

But now, even more, he wanted to catch the abaguchie and see what kind of creature it really was. With the whole town looking for it, the person who *did* catch it would be famous, practically. As famous as anyone could be in Buckman, that is.

Peter was already dancing around the box. Jake and Josh had crawled up on top to make sure Caroline didn't get out. Wally just leaned against a tree, flashlight at his side, and wondered if there was any way his own family could leave Buckman, since the Malloys certainly showed no signs of going.

"Hey, maybe the abaguchie's hungry!" Josh was saying. "Maybe we could dig up some worms and stuff them through the holes."

"Maybe the abaguchie's thirsty!" Jake said. "We could stuff the hose through one of the holes and turn it on."

"Yeah, the hose!" Josh said. "Peter, go get the hose."

"I always have to do everything!" Peter complained.

The back door slammed again. More footsteps, and Wally saw his dad coming across the backyard.

Jake and Josh slid off the crate in a hurry.

"What'd you catch?" Dad asked, coming toward the box. He glanced around at the boys. "What's under there?"

"Car-o-line!" Peter warbled.

"What?"

Jake and Josh reached down and lifted the crate while Wally shone the flashlight on it.

Caroline crawled out, eyes on the ground, and brushed off the knees of her jeans.

"Well!" said Dad, and Wally could tell he was trying not to laugh. "How was the chicken leg?"

Caroline didn't answer. Thrusting her hands in her pockets, she set off for home, looking as embarrassed as Wally had ever seen her. He *almost* felt sorry for her, but not quite.

Mr. Hatford watched her go, then turned to his sons. "Now, what was *that* all about?"

"She tried to take our bait," said Wally.

"Maybe she was hungry," offered Peter.

"Will all this never end?" asked Mr. Hatford. "Why do I get the feeling that I don't even know half of all that's been going on around here?"

" 'Cause you don't, I guess," Wally mumbled.

"That's what I thought," said their father. And then, "Come on, now, and finish your dinner."

Jake and Josh set the trap again, and then they all went inside.

•

Wally lay by the window that night, listening for the faintest clang of the cowbell. For a snort, a grunt, the slightest growl. But he heard nothing. And when he got up the next morning, he woke to the special fragrance of baking bread.

Mother had been up since five, she told them, and wanted to bake the Thanksgiving bread before she went to work at noon. She was doing the turkey, the vegetables, and the bread and coffee, and Mrs. Malloy was bringing the pies, the potatoes, and a salad.

"If I do the bread today, the vegetables tomorrow, and the turkey and dressing Thanksgiving morning, I think I'll get it all done," she said.

Wally swallowed. Thanksgiving was only two days

off? Two more days and he'd have to spend two hours looking at Caroline's face across the table? When the Bensons used to come for Thanksgiving, the guys would always do something special. The Bensons would bring a bunch of model planes, maybe, and they'd spend all Thanksgiving, before and after dinner, making models. Or maybe, if it wasn't too cold out, they'd play touch football, and their parents would come out on the back porch to watch.

Josh came down to breakfast.

"You know what I was thinking?" Mother said. "It would be nice to have place cards at the table this year. You're so good at drawing, Josh, why don't you take some index cards and make a place card for each person?"

"Place cards?" Josh yelled. "I don't want to make place cards."

"Well, you don't have to shout. I thought it would be nice to be fancy for once."

"See what's happening?" Jake said from the doorway. "We've gone from having a fun Thanksgiving to fancy. Just because the Malloys are coming over."

"*I'll* make place cards," said Peter, his mouth full of cereal.

"That will be wonderful," said Mother, raising her eyebrows at Josh, Jake, and Wally.

The only thing that made the day worth living, according to Wally, was the possibility that they might trap the abaguchie yet. He wasn't sure, but there were times he definitely believed that boys were smarter than girls. What boy would be crazy enough to crawl right into a trap and try to steal the bait without stopping to think that *he* might be trapped instead? Even Peter had brains enough not to do that.

Girls just didn't understand how things worked. They didn't think of the consequences. They just did the first dumb thing that popped in their heads, and always got into trouble. Boys thought *ahead*!

"Let's check the box before school," he said to Jake. "Maybe it fell down with*out* ringing the bell."

They put on their jackets when they were through with breakfast and went out across the yard and around the shed.

Wally stopped in his tracks and gave a shout. The refrigerator crate was gone.

Twenty-four

▽

Cruising down
the River

Caroline felt she could not go home. Screaming when she saw the yellow eyes was bad enough, but to go home now and tell Eddie that she'd been caught in the abaguchie trap? "Let me know when you think up something *really* fun," Eddie would say. Caroline couldn't blame her.

Of all the humiliating things that had happened to Caroline since she'd moved to Buckman, this had to be the worst. How on earth would she be able to face Wally and his brothers across the table at Thanksgiving?

Think, Caroline! she told herself. *You've got to be able to come up with something!*

She crossed the road and started across the swinging bridge, and by the time she reached the other side, she'd thought of something. Better than any other idea she'd had in her life.

At home she ran upstairs where Eddie was listening to a CD with earphones, and Beth was lying on her back on the floor, legs propped against the wall, a book in front of her face. Beth always read in Eddie's room when she could because her books were so scary, she hated to be alone.

Caroline went over and sat beside Eddie on the bed. She only mouthed the words because she knew Eddie couldn't hear her.

"What?" Eddie took off the earphones and looked at Caroline.

This time Caroline said it out loud, but she did not tell her sisters about being trapped. "How would you like to launch a boat?" she asked.

Eddie looked suspicious. "Launch it where?"

"On the river."

"Whose boat?"

"Guess."

Beth put down her book and sat up. "The Hatfords have a boat?"

"It's going to be," Caroline said, and told them about the abaguchie trap–refrigerator crate at the back of the Hatfords' yard, and what a wonderful boat it would make.

"Now, *that's* more like it!" said Eddie, and the girls went downstairs for their jackets.

Caroline secretly rejoiced. She'd done it! She was friends with Eddie again!

"Where are you three off to?" Mother called from the kitchen where she was making pie crusts. "I thought you might make a centerpiece out of pine cones or something to take to the Hatfords' for Thanksgiving."

"A centerpiece!" choked Eddie.

"We never had centerpieces back in Ohio. Just a bunch of relatives around the table," said Beth.

"You just never *noticed*!" said her mother. "We always had centerpieces, but I'm too busy to make one this year."

"We were going for a walk," Caroline said. "Maybe we can find some pine cones or acorns or something."

"In the dark?" said Mother.

The girls looked at each other. "We've got a flashlight," Caroline told her.

"Good. I've got some brown and orange ribbons you could use," Mother said, and brought the rolling pin down hard again on the dough.

When they got to the trees in back of the Hatfords' shed, the first thing Caroline did was detach the cowbell so it couldn't ring. Then Eddie picked up one end of the crate, and Beth and Caroline took the other end.

Slowly, step by step, they made their way softly

down the Hatfords' driveway and across the road to the river.

Caroline did not think her arms would hold up. It hadn't seemed all that heavy at first, but it was big and bulky and banged against her with every step.

She knew she was going to drop it. Was sure she was going to drop it, so to make sure she didn't, pretended she was carrying a little baby sister across a river filled with alligators. If she dropped her end of the crate, her sister, her dear little sister, her *sick* little sister, would fall into the water below and be eaten alive.

Hold on, she told herself as they crossed the road.

Hold on, she said as they made their way down the bank.

And then she heard that one marvelous word from Eddie: "Launch!" And the three girls shoved with all their might. In the darkness, the refrigerator crate drifted out into the current.

There was a small story on page six of the newspaper, which Coach Malloy read the next morning at breakfast:

Proof Inconclusive in Abaguchie Search

A tuft of brownish fur found caught in the back door of Oldakers' Bookstore after a burglar alarm was tripped Monday night is man-made fiber, forensic experts determined. With further reported sightings of the elusive creature some residents have called the abaguchie, there was speculation that this animal may have been the culprit at Oldakers', where its supposed fur was found caught in the latch.

"These are polyester fibers frequently found on outdoor wear, made to resemble fur, and have no natural properties whatsoever," said Don Matting, a forensic expert for Upshur County. . . .

Caroline exchanged looks with Beth and Eddie. That was a disappointment, because it *would* have been fun to keep the abaguchie rumor going, but right now they were more interested in whether or not the Hatford boys had discovered what happened to their trap.

They hadn't long to wait, because after they started out for school, they saw the four Hatford brothers in the middle of the swinging bridge, their mouths open, faces forlorn, staring silently at a large wooden refrigerator crate, which had somehow managed to leave their backyard in the middle of the night to throw itself into the Buckman River, and which now sat lodged against a pile of rocks in the very middle, the chicken leg still swinging from a wire on the inside.

Twenty-five

▽

Dinner Guest

Wally watched the Malloys coming up the driveway for Thanksgiving. Coach Malloy came first, holding a low open box with three pies in it, from what Wally could see.

Caroline's mother was next, holding a large covered dish. Then Eddie, who seemed to have been talked into wearing a skirt under her baseball jacket, and was carrying still another dish; Beth, who was holding a paper bag in one hand and a book stuck out in front of her with the other; and finally Caroline, with some kind of an acorn, pine-cone, ribbon creation in her hands, the ugliest thing Wally had ever seen.

The Whomper, the Weirdo, and the Crazie, that's what he and his brothers had nicknamed the girls—Whomper, because Eddie could whomp a baseball farther than any other girl he'd ever seen; Weirdo, because Beth was always reading about dragons and vampires and trolls; and Crazie, because you never knew what Caroline was going to try next, but whatever it was, it would be off the wall.

This was the first time the Bensons and Hatfords had not been together for Thanksgiving. The Benson brothers were probably sitting around a table in Georgia this very minute, their mouths full of thirty different kinds of desserts.

Well, let the Malloys come! Wally was ready for them. He fingered something in his right pants pocket, and a smile spread slowly across his face.

One minute his house was fairly quiet—the sound of a video game going in the living room, Mom in the kitchen listening to her favorite radio station, the snap of the fire in the fireplace—and the next, the hallway was filled with Malloys, with Coach Malloy's deep voice and Mrs. Malloy's high one, with the sound of hangers clunking and scraping as coats were hung in the closet.

"Happy Thanksgiving, and welcome to our home."

"How nice of you to invite us."

"A real November sky out there."

"My, those pies smell so good."

Just like it was when the Bensons used to come, there was so much food, it didn't all fit on the table. Mr. Hatford carved half the twenty-pound turkey and set the rest on the back porch, but things still didn't seem the same as when the Bensons were there.

When they sat down around the big table, with Peter's place cards at every plate, Wally sat right beside Caroline. Jake had switched his place card so he did not have to sit beside Eddie, and Josh had switched his so he did not have to sit beside Beth, but Wally had made sure that he was right beside Caroline.

He hoped that the Malloys did not insist on holding hands around the table during grace, or singing "Come Ye Thankful People, Come" or something, and was glad when his father bowed his head and said that he hoped the food before them would "nourish our good." Which was another way of saying that they should put their energies toward something useful. Finally the meal began.

The three Malloy girls didn't look any more comfortable than he did, Wally decided, but the worst was yet to come. And again he patted his pocket.

The plates were all stacked in front of Dad at the end of the table. Because the turkey platter was so heavy, it was the tradition in the Hatford family for Dad to put a little dark and a little white meat on each plate and pass it down one side of the table until it reached the person at the end. Then the next plate. When all the people on one side of the table had been served, Dad would pass plates down the other, one at a time.

Wally watched as the first plate went down the table and ended up in front of Mom. Then the next and the next. People began talking as the plates were passed, but Wally had his eye on the turkey. When all the people on the other side of the table had been served, Dad started the plates down Wally's side. Past Mrs. Malloy, then Peter, who handed the plate to Wally. As Wally took the plate, he carefully pulled his other hand from out of his pocket and deposited a worm—a small green worm he had found in the apples stored in the basement—along the edge of the plate. Then he gave it to Caroline, who set it down in front of her.

Nobody else seemed to notice. Out of the corner of his eye Wally saw Caroline glance at the turkey slices and then her eyes grew huge. Wally could not stop the smile that was taking over his face, and tucked his chin down in his shirt collar. When he looked sideways again, Caroline was staring right at him, and Wally knew that she knew. Strangely enough, she looked as though she also was trying not to laugh.

Wally could not figure it out. He thought she would shriek and pretend she was poisoned or something, but instead she just sat there calmly like the Queen of Sheba, while the worm slowly inched along the rim of her plate.

And soon Wally found out why. Because as soon as everyone had a plate of turkey, the other dishes were passed around. And as a casserole of green beans and corn came to Caroline, Wally stared as she put a little on her plate, and then, with the edge of the serving spoon, scooped up the worm and put it inside the dish, passing it on.

Mother took the dish from Caroline and put a spoonful of beans and corn on her plate and passed it to Jake, sitting across the table from Caroline. Jake took a spoonful, and there was the worm again, crawling around Jake's plate. He started to pick up his fork, then startled, and glanced over to where Wally and Caroline were grinning. Then Jake, too, smiled a little. When the sweet potatoes came around next, in went the worm and out it came again on Coach Malloy's plate.

By now Josh and Eddie could see that something was going on, and all eyes were on Coach Malloy as the worm crawled under his fork, then over his fork. Caroline's father lifted a bite to his mouth, then lowered it again as he asked a question, the worm dangling like a sky diver.

Down went the fork as Coach Malloy and Mrs. Hatford talked about the best kind of paint to use on cement, and the worm wriggled under a leaf of lettuce. By now Beth was in on the joke.

Finally Coach Malloy stabbed at his lettuce, brought the fork to his mouth, worm and all, and in it went. The three Malloy girls and Wally, Josh, and Jake stared in horror as Coach Malloy's lips closed over the hapless worm, and the big jaws began moving up and down.

Beth covered her mouth with her napkin. Jake and Wally looked wide eyed at each other. But Coach Malloy swallowed, and the worm was gone.

A grin traveled around the table, leap-frogging over the parents, who went right on talking. Wally almost felt like laughing out loud.

Maybe it wouldn't be as bad as he thought, having the girls here in Buckman. Maybe between the seven of them, they could all think up enough to do until the Bensons came back. *If* they came back. And if they didn't?

Well, when had the Benson brothers ever passed a worm from plate to plate at Thanksgiving? When had they ever thrown one of Mom's cakes in the river, probably the most awesome sight Wally had ever seen? If the Malloys weren't around, what *would* Wally and his brothers be doing? Being bored half out of their minds, that's what!

He blinked as he heard the word *abaguchie* again,

and paid attention. His parents were talking about it now with Mr. and Mrs. Malloy.

"Fellow over at the college says he thinks it's a bobcat," said the coach. "Sometimes they come close in to town when food is scarce, he says, and that's probably what people have been seeing."

Wally's dad helped himself to bread and then the butter. "Even a possum or raccoon can seem bigger at night than if you glimpse it by day," he put in.

"Frankly," said Mother, "I think it's an overactive imagination."

"I agree, Ellen," said Mrs. Malloy. "You get a rumor going about strange creatures and loud squalls in the night, and suddenly everybody's seeing and hearing things."

That wasn't what Wally wanted to hear at all. He wanted to know that it was a weird animal no one had ever seen before—some prehistoric creature that only came out every twenty years or so in West Virginia. He wanted to think that if things ever slowed down between the Hatfords and the Malloys, he'd have abaguchie stories for entertainment.

At that precise moment there was a crash, then a thud on the back porch.

Wally looked over at Jake and Josh; Caroline was staring at her sisters.

Mrs. Hatford pushed her chair away from the table. "Now, what was *that*?"

Instantly Wally was on his feet, and suddenly everyone was hurrying through the kitchen and crowding through the doorway to the back porch.

There was the roasting pan upside down on the floor, the turkey carcass nowhere in sight. And just as Wally and his brothers, and Caroline and her sisters, lifted their eyes to the yard beyond, they saw a tail, a tawny tail, dart swiftly into the trees behind the shed and, just as quickly, disappear.

"Well, for heaven's sake!" gasped Mother.

"There goes our dinner," said Dad. "I hope everyone had enough turkey, because I'm not going after that one."

"Did you get a good look?" asked Mrs. Malloy.

"It looked bigger than a bobcat to me," said the coach. "I'm no expert on these things, but I don't think that was a dog or a bobcat, either one. Maybe the abaguchie creature isn't so imaginary after all."

Mrs. Hatford sighed. "Something *else* to worry about!"

Worry? Wally looked around at his brothers. Then he looked at Caroline, Beth, and Eddie. They didn't look worried. There wasn't a worried face among them. Caroline's eyes almost snapped with excitement, and Jake and Josh looked as though they could hardly wait for dinner to be over so they could start tracking the animal. Just telling about this at school would be half the fun.

A d even as Wally went back to the table and saw that the turkey platter was empty, there was a grin that inched wormlike across his face.

About the Author

Readers of Phyllis Reynolds Naylor's boys-versus-girls books often want to know who's finally going to win the war. Well, says Naylor, she herself is a girl, but she raised two sons, so she knows how boys feel as well. Readers will just have to wait to see what the Hatfords and the Malloys have in mind.

The town of Buckman in the stories is really Buckhannon, West Virginia, where Naylor's husband spent most of his growing-up years.

Phyllis Reynolds Naylor is the author of more than a hundred books, including the Newbery Award–winning *Shiloh* and the other two books in the Shiloh trilogy, *Shiloh Season* and *Saving Shiloh*. She and her husband live in Bethesda, Maryland. They are the parents of two grown sons and have three grandchildren.